NO MORE EXCUSES

BE THE MAN GOD MADE YOU TO BE

TONY EVANS

Lifeway Press®
Nashville, Tennessee

EDITORIAL TEAM

Heather Hair
Writer

Kyle Wiltshire
Content Editor

Morgan Hawk
Production Editor

Jon Rodda
Art Director

Karen Daniel
Editorial Team Leader

John Paul Basham
Manager, Student Ministry Publishing

Ben Trueblood
Director, Student Ministry

ISBN 978-1-0877-5836-7 • Item 005836432

Dewey decimal classification: 248.842
Subject headings: RELIGION / CHRISTIAN MINISTRY / YOUTH

My deepest thanks go to Mrs. Heather Hair for her skills and insights in collaboration on this manuscript.

Printed in the United States of America

Student Ministry Publishing • Lifeway Resources • One Lifeway Plaza • Nashville, TN 37234

CONTENTS

ABOUT THE AUTHOR

DR. TONY EVANS is one of America's most respected leaders in evangelical circles. He's a pastor, a best-selling author, and a frequent speaker at Bible conferences and seminars throughout the nation. He has served as the senior pastor of Oak Cliff Bible Fellowship for more than forty years, witnessing its growth from ten people in 1976 to more than ten thousand with more than one hundred ministries.

Dr. Evans also serves as the president of The Urban Alternative, a national ministry that seeks to restore hope and transform lives through the proclamation and application of God's Word. His daily radio broadcast, *The Alternative with Dr. Tony Evans,* can be heard on more than 1,400 radio outlets throughout the United States and in more than 130 countries.

Dr. Evans holds the honor of writing and publishing the first full-Bible commentary and study Bible by an African American. A former chaplain for the Dallas Cowboys, he's currently the chaplain for the NBA's Dallas Mavericks, a team he has served for more than thirty years.

Through his local church and national ministry, Dr. Evans has set in motion a kingdom-agenda philosophy of ministry that teaches God's comprehensive rule over every area of life, as demonstrated through the individual, family, church, and society.

Dr. Evans was married to Lois, his wife and ministry partner for nearly fifty years, before her passing in 2019. They are the proud parents of four—Chrystal, Priscilla, Anthony Jr., and Jonathan—and have a number of grandchildren.

ABOUT THE URBAN ALTERNATIVE

The Urban Alternative (TUA) is a Christian broadcast and teaching ministry founded more than thirty-five years ago by Dr. Tony Evans. TUA seeks to promote a kingdom-agenda philosophy designed to enable people to live all of life underneath the comprehensive rule of God. This is accomplished through a variety of means, including media, resources, ministries, and community-impact training.

HOW TO GET THE MOST FROM THIS STUDY

This Bible-study book includes eight weeks of content for group and personal study.

GROUP SESSIONS

Regardless of what day of the week your group meets, each week of content begins with the group session. Each session uses the following format to facilitate simple yet meaningful interaction among students, with God's Word, and with the teaching of Dr. Evans.

START. This page includes questions to get the conversation started and to introduce the video teaching.

WATCH. Use the fill-in-the-blanks from Dr. Evans's teaching so students can follow along as they watch the video.

MAN UP. This page includes questions and statements that guide the group to respond to Dr. Evans's video teaching and to relevant Bible passages.

PERSONAL STUDY

Each week provides three days of Bible study and learning activities for individual engagement between group sessions.

DAY 1: HIT THE STREETS. This section highlights practical steps for taking the week's teaching and putting it into practice.

DAYS 2-3: These personal studies go deeper into the sessions, revisiting stories, Scriptures, and themes Dr. Evans introduced in the videos and in your group time, so students can understand and apply what they've learned on a deeper level. Students should use the other days of the week to reflect on what God is teaching them and to practice putting the biblical principles into action.

D-GROUP GUIDES

In addition to the group sessions and personal studies, D-Group guides are provided at the back of this Bible-study book. These guides correspond to the eight weeks of study and are designed to be used in a smaller group of three or four for deeper discussion and accountability. Each week's guide includes a devotional written by one of Dr. Evans's sons, Anthony or Jonathan, as well as a guide for smaller group discussion. Each guide provides helpful thoughts on the week's content and suggests a few questions for discussion and accountability among the group.

TIPS FOR LEADING A SMALL GROUP

Follow these tips to prepare for each group session.

PRAYERFULLY PREPARE

REVIEW. Review the weekly video, teaching material, and group questions ahead of time in order be best prepared for your time with your guys.

PRAY. Be intentional about praying for each person in the group. Ask the Holy Spirit to work through you and the group discussion as you point to Jesus each week through God's Word.

MINIMIZE DISTRACTIONS

Create an environment that doesn't distract. Ask students not to use their phones and to bring a physical Bible. Plan ahead by considering these details, include seating, temperature, lighting, snacks, and general cleanliness. While most young men aren't terribly concerned with these things (other than snacks), it will help them not be distracted. Do everything in your ability to help students focus on what's most important: connecting with God, the Bible, and each other.

ENCOURAGE DISCUSSION

A good small-group experience has the following characteristics.

EVERYONE IS INCLUDED. Your goal is to foster a community in which guys are welcome just as they are but encouraged to grow spiritually. Always be aware of opportunities to include any students who visit the group and to invite new guys to join your group.

EVERYONE PARTICIPATES. Encourage everyone to ask questions, share responses, or read aloud.

NO ONE DOMINATES—NOT EVEN THE LEADER. Be sure that your time speaking as a leader takes up less than half of your time together as a group. Politely guide discussion if anyone dominates.

NOBODY IS RUSHED THROUGH QUESTIONS. Don't feel that a moment of silence is a bad thing. Students often need time to think about their responses to questions they've just heard or to gain courage to share what God is stirring in their hearts.

INPUT IS AFFIRMED AND FOLLOWED UP. Make sure you point out something true or helpful in a response. Don't just move on. Build community with follow-up questions, asking how other people have experienced similar things or how a truth has shaped their understanding of God and the Scripture you're studying. People are less likely to speak up if they fear that you don't actually want to hear their answers or that you're looking for only a certain answer.

GOD AND HIS WORD ARE CENTRAL. Opinions and experiences can be helpful, but God has given us the truth. Trust God's Word to be the authority and God's Spirit to work in people's lives. You can't change anyone, but God can. Continually point students to the Word and to active steps of faith.

KEEP CONNECTING

Think of ways to connect with students during the week. Participation during the group session is always improved when guys spend time connecting with one another outside the group sessions. The more people are comfortable with and involved in one another's lives, the more they'll look forward to being together. When people move beyond being friendly to truly being friends who form a community, they come to each session eager to engage instead of just attending.

ENCOURAGE STUDENTS with thoughts, commitments, or questions from the session by connecting through these communication channels: texts, social media, and schools visits (where permissible).

BUILD DEEPER FRIENDSHIPS by planning or spontaneously inviting group members to join you outside your regularly scheduled group time for activities like these: meals, fun activities, and projects around your school, church or community.

NO MORE EXCUSES

BE THE MAN GOD MADE YOU TO BE!

TONY EVANS

SESSION 1

NO MORE HIDING BEHIND THE PAST

START

Welcome to Session 1 of *No More Excuses.*

Welcome to *No More Excuses.* In this Bible study we're going to identify and overcome the excuses men, young, old, and everywhere in between, use to keep from being the people God has called them to be. We'll begin by looking at the past.

Good or bad, what's an event in your past that you often think about?

Even though you are young, your past is made up of the good, the bad, and the ugly. Many of your experiences have been positive, but many have also been bad or painful. Painful pasts come in all shapes, sizes, and degrees of intensity. Like it or not, your past often influences your present.

What's an example of something from your past that influences the way you live in the present?

What can you do to overcome the negative influences of your past? The Bible has a lot to teach us on this subject. Let's watch Session 1, where we'll explore the life of Joseph, a man who overcame a lot of obstacles and opposition to rise to a position of great power, authority, and influence for God's purposes in the world.

Ask someone to pray before watching the video teaching.

WATCH

NOTE: In these videos Dr. Evans will refer to the guys in your group as "men" no matter what stage of manhood they are in. Use this to encourage them to begin rising to the level of manhood in their hearts and minds. Even though they are still teens, encourage them to see Dr. Evans's teaching as a building block toward manhood in their lives.

Fill in the blanks to follow along as you watch video Session 1.

God does not want us to make _____ for the failures in our lives. He wants us to take _____ .

We can no longer hide behind the_____. We can no longer let _____ define us.

We men need God to deliver us from _____ because too many of us are chained to _____.

God wants to deliver us from the _____ taking the _____ has done in our lives.

God can take your _____and turn it into an awesome _____.

Forgiving does not mean you don't _____it happened. It means you're no longer seeking _____because it happened.

God can take the mess of _____ and turn it into the miracle of _____.

"You meant evil against me, but God meant it for good."
GENESIS 50:20

MAN UP

Use the following guide and questions
to discuss the video teaching.

Read Genesis 50:20.

Joseph embraced his past because he recognized that God had used it to turn around his present and give him a productive future. Joseph made this statement found in Genesis 50:20 when he was second in command of Egypt and was clearly fulfilling God's plan for himself and for the survival of the nation of Israel. To be honest, he was already on top. But God has called us to live according to this truth even when we haven't yet seen Him turn our circumstances around. He asks us to do that by faith.

What makes it harder to live out the truth of Genesis 50:20 before we've seen God turn our situation around?

What are some of the benefits of embracing the truth of Genesis 50:20 in full faith and in spite of our circumstances?

In sports you've probably seen a player start limping after making a bad play. Then, minutes later, you notice their limp is gone. Why is this? The player is hoping that the limp will offer them an excuse for the bad play. Then after the play is forgotten, so is the limp. A player uses that kind of limp, what Dr. Evans's called a loser's limp, to imply that he failed because of an injury, not through any fault of his own.

The limp is an excuse. It implies that if the player had been at full capacity, he would have made the play. It's meant to draw attention away from the failure of the present by directing that attention to an excuse that came before it.

In what ways might guys use this loser's limp excuse in everyday life?

In the video Dr. Evans said, "God does not want us to make excuses for the failures in our lives. He wants us to take responsibility and ownership. That means we can no longer hide behind the past. We can no longer let yesterday define us." Injury or not, painful past or not, God opposes the use of negative situations in our lives as excuses for personal failures. We have to own our failures, get up, and move forward.

What does it look like to own a personal setback or challenge in the present instead of making an excuse for it?

Dr. Evans used the example of an enormous adult elephant staying chained to a small stake due to its memory of the past. As a younger, less powerful elephant, it couldn't pull away from the stake. As an adult, it could easily get loose, but the memory of the past keeps the older, stronger elephant chained because the chain convinces the animal it can't break free.

Name common mindsets that hold guys back from fully living out their strength in Christ and continuing to dwell in the past.

All of us have gone through difficult experiences. Joseph's example is unique but he is not alone in having challenging days. Joseph got through those hard days by recognizing that God was with him. God is with you as well. And He didn't abandon you during the challenging experiences of your past.

Dr. Evans said Joseph had to forgive yesterday. This meant no longer seeking revenge, sulking, or staring at the past, but trusting that God knew how to turn it around for good.

Do you need to forgive someone or something? It might even be yourself. What are benefits of forgiveness that you learned from the video teaching?

PRAYER

Close the session with prayer.

Father, in a world full of excuses, You've asked us to rise above them and live with personal responsibility and ownership. Help each of us identify past hurts and experiences we need to let go of, forgive, and see in the light of Your power and purpose. Help us live as young men without excuses as we trust in Your ability to transform our lives. In Christ's name, amen.

DAY 1
HIT THE STREETS

THREE STEPS TO WINNING THE RACE

Every Thanksgiving the Evans family takes part in what's known as the Turkey Trot. This 5K run/walk brings thousands of people together with the goal of raising funds for the Dallas YMCA. In this race, simply finishing is winning because all proceeds go to a good cause. But not so for competitive races. Most races award a first-place finisher with a medal, trophy, or another symbol of victory. In those races, coming in fifth, tenth, or one-hundredth is never the goal. Athletes train and compete in order to come in first.

Paul pictured the Christian life as a race. He wrote:

> Do you not know that those who run in a
> race all run, but only one receives the prize?
> Run in such a way that you may win.
> 1 CORINTHIANS 9:24

Following these three strategic steps can help you accomplish your goals and develop a passion to be a winner for God.

1. GO FOR THE GOLD

A nice track suit doesn't make you a runner, just as wearing a football jersey doesn't make you an NFL player. To go for the gold, you need to do more than be a part of the pack. Never settle for simply getting on the field or in the race. Run to win! The glory of God, for all who know Him, is eternal and unfading. One day God is going to reward you for what you do for Him. Because of the nature of that reward, pursue "the upward call of God in Christ Jesus" (Phil. 3:14) with all you have. Living a life filled with excuses keeps you from pursing the finish line with passion and intensity equal to the stakes of your eternal race.

2. KEEP YOUR EYE ON THE PRIZE

Athletes who compete take part in strict training. Strict training and hard work are just that—hard. They're disciplines you have to make yourself do. Unless you stay focused on the *why* behind the *what,* you might quit.

There is an Olympic gold medalist who attends Dr. Evans's church. He's known her since she was a kid. The hours, days, weeks, and months she put into preparing for the Olympics were possible only because she kept her eye on the prize. Every decision she made in the years leading up to her gold medal was influenced by that one pursuit. We ought to pursue God's eternal prize with no less effort.

Young kingdom men must train daily in godliness, invest in the eternal, seek to spend time with the Lord in prayer and Bible study, serve others, and give sacrificially of themselves to the cause of the kingdom.

3. REMOVE DISTRACTIONS

The writer of Hebrews expressed the last step this way:

> Let us lay aside every hindrance and the
> sin that so easily ensnares us.
> HEBREWS 12:1, CSB

What's distracting you? In what ways are you spending your time on things that aren't of eternal value? Get rid of it. Stop watching it. Stop talking to them. Stop going there. Whatever stands in the way of fully living out God's plan and gaining victory over sin ought to have no place in your life.

LACE 'EM UP

Go for the gold this week. Identify one element of your life that is keeping you from pursuing your relationship with God whole-heartedly and eliminate it from your life. Keep your eyes on the prize by removing the distractions!

DAY 2
IF YOU'RE NOT DEAD, GOD'S NOT DONE

Various passages in the Bible picture the Christian life as a race or other athletic competition (see 1 Tim. 4:7-8; Gal. 5:7; Heb. 12:1; James 1:12). Both require attention and effort. Both require sacrifice and perseverance. Both have a clearly defined finish line to strive for. The finish line of this study is to become a young kingdom man—a young man who places himself under God's control and submits his life to the Lordship of Jesus Christ. A young kingdom man lives according to God's rule. Now that you have a goal in mind, let's begin making strides toward the finish line.

Unlike athletic competition, the race for the Christian lasts a lifetime. If you're not dead, you aren't finished yet. You still have time to push forward in the race and win. You may be coming to the starting blocks with regrets over personal or spiritual failure. You may have stumbled coming out of the blocks. You may have tripped during the race. You may even be starting the race a little late, but God can help you make up for lost time. He can help you pick up speed and make up ground.

Read the following verse and answer the questions.

> I am confident of this very thing, that He who began a good work in you will perfect it until the day of Christ Jesus.
> PHILIPPIANS 1:6

What confidence comes from knowing that God began and will complete the work in your life?

Our relationship with God begins with God. Paul was saying that what God starts, He finishes. What God initiates, He completes. God wants us to be involved in His mission in the world to make Himself known by making His people more like His Son. He always helps us finish. Sometimes it may appear that God is doing nothing and everything is up to us. Yet God is constantly working behind the scenes to lead us toward the finish line.

How do you rest in the confidence that God will carry out His work in your life from start to finish? How should this assurance influence your emotions, prayers, and actions?

Paul knew how to persevere. He knew how to let go of the past. Paul had a dark past. He persecuted and oppressed the church. But one day Jesus met him on the road to Damascus. That encounter changed Paul's life. He knew the wisdom of forgetting failures and even successes. He wrote about it in Philippians 3. Paul pressed on:

> Brothers, I do not consider myself to have taken hold
> of it. But one thing I do: Forgetting what is behind and
> reaching forward to what is ahead, I pursue as my goal the
> prize promised by God's heavenly call in Christ Jesus.
> PHILIPPIANS 3:13-14 (HCSB)

What failures from you past are you holding on to and using as an excuse?

You may not be able to completely forget your past, but in what ways can you follow Paul's example of "forgetting what is behind" and looking forward to what's ahead?

Paul had a kingdom-man attitude. He let go of the things that were behind him. His eyes were straight ahead, focused on the goal. Runners don't win a race looking backward. They have to keep their eyes on the finish line. You can't change yesterday, but you can do a lot about what happens tomorrow. Don't let other people stop you from running for God. Don't let other people distract you from seeking His approval.

The truth is that if you know Jesus, you already have God's approval. When you believed the gospel, God exchanged all the sin in your past, present, and future, for the perfect life of His Son. You're now in Christ, so when God sees you, He doesn't see your past; He sees Jesus' perfect record. God isn't concerned about your past failures; however, He has an unmistakable and amazing way of using even failure to bring about success.

Often we spend too much time focusing on what other people think about us and allow it to hold us back. Why is it important to focus only on God and His view of you instead of what others think about you?

God has a purpose for your life, a destiny for you to live out, a plan that He uniquely created you to fulfill. You advance toward that goal by focusing each day on aligning your thoughts, attitudes, and behavior with His Word and His will. Be faithful in the small things, and He will put you in charge of many things (see Matt. 25:21). If you drop a pass or miss a tackle, don't blame others. Don't fake a limp. Get back up; admit your failure to God, trusting in His provision for your forgiveness (the Bible calls this step repentance); let it go; and move forward in the knowledge that your past doesn't define you. Because you're accepted and forgiven, you're living under God's approval.

Living in God's approval allows us to bear spiritual fruit, which is the outward evidence that we're being inwardly changed by God's work in our lives. For example, when a guy lifts weights, the hours in the gym show up as muscles begin to develop and his body responds to the work it has endured. Similarly, spiritual sculpting takes place when you let go of your past and take responsibility for your sins and your spiritual development. Fruit can include greater patience, tolerance, self-control, love, diligence, leadership, wisdom, grace, and a ton of other traits and actions that lead to eternal rewards.

Why would an unhealthy fixation on our past keep us from bearing fruit in the present?

Why is it important that we bear fruit after repenting of sin? What does it reveal if we don't?

For Paul, bearing fruit was rooted in self-control. He wrote:

> Everyone who competes in the games exercises self-control in all things. They then do it to receive a perishable wreath, but we an imperishable. Therefore I run in such a way, as not without aim; I box in such a way, as not beating the air; but I discipline my body and make it my slave, so that, after I have preached to others, I myself will not be disqualified.
> 1 CORINTHIANS 9:25-27

The best athletes exhibit self-control. The Greek word Paul used for *self-control* in verse 25 referred to athletes in his day who abstained from unhealthy food, alcohol, and sex prior to competition. These athletes understood the need for their bodies to be at full capacity for victory. They were willing to invest in themselves to win the prize set before them.

The prize in the Christian life is in the future. Hiding behind the past is harmful because it focuses our attention in the wrong place. It causes us to feel shame and guilt over past failings instead of resting in the approval we have in Jesus and in the confidence that comes from knowing He will finish the work He began. We need to exercise diligence and self-control to let go of the past.

What's one area of your life in which you're willing to exercise self-control in order to have a greater capacity for spiritual focus and commitment?

PRAY

Pray about your personal commitment to God and His expression of greatness through you. Ask Him to give you a glimpse of His plans for your future and to inspire you on your path of spiritual development. Ask for His help in reducing distractions that keep you from fully pursuing Him. Thank Him for the work He has begun in your life and ask Him to increase your faith and bring it to completion.

DAY 3
CROWN ME

Ever played checkers? Once you're able to move a checker to the other side of the board, you get to say, "King me." That means your checker is rewarded with all of the rights and privileges of the crown. Now that you're wearing a crown, you can move forward or backwards around the board, and your odds of winning increase

The kingdom life comes with its own rewards as well. When you obtain these, either in time or in eternity, you're entitled to all of the rights and privileges they supply. Scripture calls them crowns. Today we'll look at five of them.

As a young kingdom man, you have all it takes to obtain each of these crowns. You just need to pursue them the way God has instructed. But I have to point out that it won't be easy. Unlike compliments in our culture, crowns don't come cheap. The crowns the Bible describes are different from earthly treasure, which is subject to decay and corruption.

Read Jesus's words in Matthew 6:19-21.

Describe the difference between treasure on earth and treasure in heaven.

THE CROWN OF MASTERY. The first crown is the crown of mastery, the reward for faithful obedience, which we've already read about in 1 Corinthians 9:24-25. You win this crown by committing to discipline in order to compete successfully. No one ever becomes good at anything without disciplining himself. Maybe you've heard of the ten-thousand-hour rule that Malcolm Gladwell made famous.[1] The principle is that it requires ten thousand hours of doing something again and again until you master it. Although ten thousand hours may not be the exact requirement, the point is that consistency creates competency, and competency leads to mastery. You must be consistent in your spiritual walk and development over a long period of time in order to win this crown.

Read 1 Corinthians 9:24-25. How can you become more consistent in your spiritual development?

We develop spiritually by engaging in spiritual disciplines like Bible reading, prayer, fasting, giving, serving, and others. Which of these do you struggle with the most? How will you grow in your mastery of this discipline?

THE CROWN OF REJOICING. In 1 Thessalonians 2:19, we're told about our next crown—the crown of rejoicing. This crown is associated with faithfulness in the work of evangelism. God will honor those who made winning others to Christ the passion of their lives. It's good for you as a young kingdom man to stop regularly and take inventory of how often you have gospel conversations with others.

Read 1 Thessalonians 2:19. When was the most recent time you talked to someone about Jesus?

With whom could you share your faith this week? How are you building that relationship?

THE CROWN OF GLORY. The third crown is the crown of glory, given for faithfulness in discipleship. The apostle Peter described this crown in 1 Peter 5:2-4. The idea of discipling is to lead someone in such a way that he desires to follow you in your Christian walk. According to Peter, those who lead others to maturity in Christ will be rewarded. They'll be put in God's hall of fame.

Dr. Evans visited the NFL headquarters in New York when he filmed for the feature documentary *Kingdom Men Rising*. On one of the upper floors was a magnificent display cabinet running the length of the room. Behind glass was displayed each Super Bowl ring going back to the beginning of the game. Also displayed was the Lombardi Trophy. It was a sight to see! Although these treasures will fade one day, the display case of your discipleship in eternity will last forever. If you're a young man who desires to disciple others, people will see your rewards in heaven and say, "Wow!"

Read 1 Peter 5:2-4. Who has or is discipling you? What did you learn from them?

What are some ways you can help disciple others even as a teenager?

THE CROWN OF LIFE. The risen Christ told the church in Smyrna about this crown.

Read Revelation 2:10.

Some young men seem to go from one trial to another. God says your hardship doesn't go unnoticed in heaven. You endure when you refuse to throw in the towel and make excuses. When this is your practice, God has a crown waiting for you. If you hang in there through suffering, knowing God is working His purposes in your life, even if you don't know exactly all He's doing, you'll receive this crown.

Identify times in your life when you've thrown in the towel because it got too hard.

Now repent and make a plan to begin pursuing Christ's purpose for you in this area of your life. If you can't recall giving up, thank God for His faithfulness in seeing you through difficult times and ask Him to give you strength to continue.

THE CROWN OF RIGHTEOUSNESS. The crown of righteousness is given for faithfulness in ministry. Described in 2 Timothy 4:7-8, it comes through keeping the faith all the way to the end.

The good news about all five of these crowns is that you don't have to know a special secret to qualify for them. They aren't just for super-saints. Receiving them is a matter of everyday, consistent faithfulness, of getting up every morning and saying, "Lord, I give You my life today. I want to obey You and to honor You in everything I say and do."

It's important for us to realize that these crowns await us in the future. However, to receive them, we must be faithful in the present. Continuing to hide behind our past will keep us from living in the present and from looking toward the future. All of these crowns are attainable as Christ works in and through your life. He's the goal; He awards us these crowns as we faithfully pursue Him.

> **Read 2 Timothy 4:7-8. How does the hope of a future reward in heaven help us remain faithful in the present? Why does faithfulness require us to let go of our past?**

> **How does knowing that these crowns come as we faithfully pursue Christ help you to lead a genuine and authentic life before God?**

PRAY

Pray and commit your day, week, and year to Christ.
Submit to Him and ask Him to help you pursue Him
with all your heart, soul, mind and strength.

NO MORE EXCUSES

BE THE MAN GOD MADE YOU TO BE!

TONY EVANS

SESSION 2
NO MORE HOLDING BACK

START

Welcome to Session 2 of *No More Excuses*.

Last week looked at how events from the past can keep us from moving forward to become the young kingdom men God is calling us to be.

When are you most likely to dwell on the past?

This week we're going to be encouraged to stop holding back and take responsibility. When a football team gathers in a circle before a game on its home field, a familiar phrase often comes out: "This is our house!" With these words the team states its intention to fiercely defend its turf from the opposing team. This mindset often propels the team to a victory even though it may not be favored to win.

How do we as believers defend our "turf" from the enemy?

How does knowing that you belong to Christ give you a "home field advantage" over the enemy?

God has given each man—even young men—an opportunity to influence, whether with his friends, family, school, church, or other extracurricular activities. This opportunity to influence also connects to his personal life, emotions, and development. This week's teaching highlights an episode from Elisha's ministry and issues a call for you to live boldly while overcoming any efforts the enemy may use to hold you back.

Ask someone to pray before watching the video teaching.

WATCH

NOTE: Remember Dr. Evans's call to manhood for your guys. He's not holding back. He's calling them to a higher standard and level of maturity.

Fill in the blanks to follow along as you watch video Session 2.

Claim a _____ you do not yet see and you do not yet have.

We're going to hand the ball off to God, but we're going to do what we need to do to make sure we are _____ in the _____ God wants to bring.

God works out things in the _____ before He reveals them in the _____.

If you've dropped some passes in the first _____, this is the time to get _____ and not hold _____.

Far too many are waiting on _____ when _____ is waiting on us.

God has given you _____ to handle the _____ that come.

I'm going to give God _____ I've got because I'm going to give God _____ to work with.

When you do it God's way and start with your spiritual commitment first, He brings heaven's pleasure into your pain, into your _____, into your frustrations, into your _____.

The only time you stop is when God stops you, not when you _____ yourself.

MAN UP

Use the following questions to discuss the video teaching.

Read the following verse together.

Elisha said to him, "Take a bow and arrows."
So he took a bow and arrows.
2 KINGS 13:15

As the prophet Elisha was dying, the king of Israel, Joash, was distraught. Joash was acting like a frightened child instead of like a confident king. Elisha commanded the king to do something unusual; pick up the bow and shoot arrows to mark God's victory. Joash shot three arrows and then stopped. Elisha confronted Joash's lack of confidence. He could have shot more arrows but decided to stop with three.

God is calling young men to pick up the tools He has given them and use them. God is raising up a generation who won't hold back. He wants us to have a dominant spirit. That doesn't mean to dominate in a hurtful way but rather to recognize the divine authority given to us by the Lord in order to execute God's plans and purposes on earth. We've been assigned to bring heaven's rule into history.

How could a wrong understanding of dominance reduce or remove many young men's desires to boldly live out their faith?

What did Joash miss by holding back? What have you missed?

In the video Dr. Evans used the example of leaving in the middle of a game and going into the stands to describe guys who hold back from living out their kingdom calling. Far too many guys start off strong, only to throw in the towel midway through when emotions, relationships, or pressures from the world become difficult. Examples could include pursuing a dream to go to college, investing in friendships, spending time in God's Word, accountability with other guys, investing in younger students, growing in Christ, praying, and many other areas of life.

What types of challenges contribute to a guy's decision to throw in the towel?

In the video Dr. Evans said, "Worse than leaving the fields and going up into the stands, men have decided to become spectators so that somebody else can solve the problem. Yet God has created them to get on the field and to call this His house."

What does it look like for young men to live like all of creation is God's house? Give an example in each of these areas of a guy's everyday life: relationships with the opposite sex, family, church, school, and friends.

The biblical account of Elisha's instruction for King Joash to shoot an arrow out the window came with a unique twist. That twist involved the prophet laying his hands on the king's hands (see 2 Kings 13:16). This display of assistance served as a reminder to the king where his true power came from and where he would find his victory. God supplied power to the king to the extent that the king obeyed and relied on God.

How do guys seek to gain their own victories in life without relying on God's power or without completely obeying His will?

The king's half-hearted obedience in shooting only three arrows into the ground disqualified him from complete victory over his enemy. The king held back some of his resources instead of trusting in complete faith God's word through the prophet. Total obedience brings about total victory. Holding back only hurts yourself.

How do we sometimes rationalize holding back rather than living boldly with total obedience and complete faith?

PRAYER

Close the session with prayer.

Father, make us people who hold nothing back. Let us leave our all on the field of our pursuits for Your kingdom. We want to trust You fully, follow You completely, and watch You gain victories in our lives. Put us in the game and let us live out the entirety of Your purposes for us. In Christ's name, amen.

DAY I
HIT THE STREETS

GO GET IT!

God has given us more than five thousand promises in Scripture, but He's not going to force anyone to live in the victory of His fulfilled promises. You have to go get them. When the people of Israel entered the promised land, God promised their leader, Joshua, that He would be given any piece of land where his foot walked (see Josh. 1:3), but he had to go get it. He couldn't stay where he was and simply claim victory.

Here are four key principles for claiming the promises God has made.

I. LEAVE THE PAST BEHIND

Learn from yesterday; don't live in it. As Joshua set out to take the Israelites on a military conquest across the land, he had to let go of Moses as the leader and commander. The miracles Moses had performed for the Israelite people were in the past. God would use a new man and a new plan to secure the nation's victories moving forward. Letting go of the past was critical for their progress.

2. SEIZE YOUR SPIRITUAL INHERITANCE

Joshua had to take steps of faith to secure the promises God had made. God placed a condition on receiving His victories. Joshua had to go places where he might normally have been afraid to go. Doing so required faith. Passively waiting for God to dump spiritual promises onto you isn't the way God operates. You have to act in faith and obedience.

3. FOCUS ON GOD, NOT PEOPLE

God promised Joshua:

> No man will be able to stand before you all the days
> of your life. Just as I have been with Moses, I will
> be with you; I will not fail you or forsake you.
> JOSHUA 1:5

No doubt Joshua faced intimidating and powerful enemies as he sought to conquer the promised land. But God assured him of victory. If Joshua had focused on the people in his way, he might have cowered in fear. Likewise, when you direct your focus on God and His Word, you can reduce the fear and doubt in your life.

4. STAY TIED TO GOD'S WORD

A critical element in Joshua's conquests was his consistency in staying tied to God's Word. God instructed him:

> Only be strong and very courageous; be careful to
> do according to all the law which Moses My servant
> commanded you; do not turn from it to the right or to
> the left, so that you may have success wherever you go.
> JOSHUA 1:7

God's Word gives wisdom on what to do, when to do it, and how to gain spiritual victories in spite of physical limitations or obstacles. As you move forward in life, meditate on and apply the truths of Scripture, and you'll gain insight and guidance for accomplishing what God has in store for you.

LACE 'EM UP

Go get it this week! Memorize Joshua 1:9. Every time you feel a sense of fear creeping into your heart quote it. Tell yourself, "be strong and courageous." Know that staying tied to God's Word will fuel you through your days and will help you become the young kingdom man He has designed you to be. And guess what? Young kingdom men one day become old kingdom men when they continue to walk with God all their days.

DAY 2
THE FIXER-UPPER

When you see something broken, do you long to fix it? Maybe you feel a loose doorknob and examine it to try to make it right again. Or you see your friend with a jacked up jump shot and you want to give him some pointers on how to straighten out that shooting stroke. We like to fix things; it's how God made us. He created us to cultivate, redeem, and restore, so desiring to fix things is in our nature. It's what we long to do.

However, no one can fix things like God. God has as many methods of fixing things as there are stars in the sky. He's the great un-figure-out-able God. He knows how to turn things that are upside-down, right side up. He can turn around life situations on a dime and heal wounds that have festered for years. The problem comes when we resist His method for doing it. Issues arise when we think we know better than God how to fix what He's already fixing Himself.

Read Joshua 3:1-13 before answering the following questions.

What did God promise Joshua He would do when the priests stood in the water?

What kind of faith must it have taken for the priests to obey Joshua's orders as they crossed the Jordan? What would have happened if they had held back?

Joshua's directions must have been shocking to the priests. The Bible doesn't tell us, but they may have been tempted to hold back. Holding back happens when we fail to trust God and His plans. We falsely believe that because His plans don't make sense to us, they don't make sense at all. Holding back keeps us from experiencing all God has for us. Our best moments happen when we refuse to hold back and begin taking steps of faith.

In Joshua 3 it wasn't immediately clear that God would part the Jordan by faith. God rarely tells us the *how* because He wants us to walk by faith and not by sight. In addition, if God told us the *how*, we might argue with Him. After all, few of us have the faith of Joshua, who was willing to walk around an enemy's walled city for seven days, open and vulnerable to attack (see Joshua. 6). Most of us would have told God He was crazy and asked if there was an alternative plan of attack. Joshua had the faith to obey God because he had witnessed God's unusual activity in his life time and time again. He didn't withhold his obedience. Instead, he trusted God and moved in faith.

Has God ever asked you to do something that didn't make sense? What was the result? How does this experience keep you from holding back in the future?

Hebrews 11:1 tells us that faith is "the proof of things not seen." How can something be unseen and real at the same time?

How should this reality affect your choices?

As a pastor, Dr. Evans is regularly asked by guys in difficult situations how God will show up and transform their challenge. His answer is always the same: "I don't know, but I know this: when God tells you to cross the Jordan, you'd better start walking and let Him work it out."

As we read in the biblical accounts, God rarely starts working out a dilemma until He sees you do what He has asked you to do. God responds when you walk by faith, not when you wish by faith. You can't exercise faith on the couch. A couch might be good for watching Netflix or playing a video game, but it doesn't take you anywhere. A couch is comfortable, but far too many guys are satisfied with being comfortable.

Describe the difference between talking by faith and walking by faith.

Why is it important to take steps of faith when God urges you to?

We can be creatures of habit. If we find a successful way to do something, we often continue it, even if it doesn't work the second time around. Long-term success requires adapting and changing. Coaches who don't know how to make changes in their approaches often don't keep their jobs very long. In fact, the teams that win the most are the ones that adapt to the opponents they face the best. Likewise, God isn't a "push, play, and go" kind of God. He varies His approach based on the circumstances and personalities of the moment.

Read the following verses.

> David inquired of the LORD, saying, "Shall I go up against the Philistines? Will You give them into my hand?" And the LORD said to David, "Go up, for I will certainly give the Philistines into your hand."
> 2 SAMUEL 5:19

> When David inquired of the LORD, He said, "You shall not go directly up; circle around behind them and come at them in front of the balsam trees."
> 2 SAMUEL 5:23

Describe the difference in approach between the two battle plans.

God is anything but predictable. He may lead you one way in a situation and a totally different way in a similar situation. Though the variables may not have changed, God will choose an alternative approach.

In the first battle David was to pursue the enemy head-on. In the second round David was to circle around behind the enemy. This example illustrates why it's critical to stay close to God, keeping the communication channels open, to keep your heart, mind, and body pure, and your sins regularly repented of so that you can hear what He has to say.

Why is it important to listen closely to God's leading and not assume He's asking you to use the same approach over and over again?

What step of faith is God asking you to take that you've been delaying? What would it look like to walk in faith instead of holding back?

How will you cultivate your sensitivity to God and His leading this week?

PRAY

Pray about an area of your life or in your circle of influence that you feel needs to be fixed. Ask God to replace your thinking on how to fix it with His. Then ask Him to give you courage to take steps of faith in doing what He has asked. Invite Him to amaze you with His involvement and victory in this specific situation.

DAY 3
LET GO

When God called people to do something spectacular in the Bible, the tasks He called them to do were typically larger than themselves. He called Abraham, who was childless at the time, to be a mighty nation. He called David, who was about your age, to single-handedly defeat someone twice his size with a stone. He called Moses, who was 80 years old, to part the Red Sea. Often you'll know it's God who's asking you to do something if it's something you can't do on your own. In fact, you can't discover how big God is unless what you need is something bigger than you can handle. And when God accomplishes what you never could have done on your own, He alone gets the glory. But to see God work this way, you have to let go of your own strategy, skills, and successes and tap into His.

When was a time in your life when God did something that was bigger than you could ever imagine?

Moses delivered his people from slavery. He led them through treacherous terrain. He performed miracles in God's name. But he never made it into the promised land. Seems harsh, doesn't it? Not really. Moses had been used so much by God that he started doing what too many of us do. He started believing the headlines and the social media comments. Then he took matters into his own hands, and as a result, he had to pay the price.

Read about the two instances when God brought water from a rock during Moses's leadership of the Israelites. These are found in Exodus 17:6 and Numbers 20:8-12.

What differences do you see between God's instructions in these instances? Why do you think those differences were important?

Moses may have given himself too much credit the first time God used him to bring water from a rock. Maybe he had a flair for the dramatic the second time around. Whatever the case, he disobeyed God and refused to let go of his ego. He struck the rock instead of simply speaking to it as God commanded. As a result, Moses lost the opportunity to complete his legacy. His pride caused him to disobey God. As a result, he lost the opportunity to go into the promised land.

Why does ego sometimes get in the way of total obedience to God?

In what ways does our world feed our egos?

A healthy identity and self-esteem are important in life. When you're rooted and grounded in Christ, you should feel confident and assured of what He can do both in and through you. But there's a fine line between healthy self-esteem and an overinflated ego. Once you cross that line, you may be tempted to toss a little of your own wisdom into God's solution to your situation. Embracing worldly wisdom causes you to hold back from fully obeying God because you foolishly believe you can do it on your own.

Have you ever found yourself overwhelmed by a situation when there seemed to be no earthly solution? What did you do?

It seems that men, young, old, and everywhere in between, are fighting more battles today than ever before. And too many are losing. Whether in their relationships, school, family, pornography, addictions, loneliness, or other overwhelming struggles, many guys today are fighting a losing battle against sin. Concerned about the attacks they're facing, they go to God for His wisdom and His strategy. And they apply it. But only some of it.

Ego and an unwillingness to be vulnerable can cause a guy to hold back and fall short of all God has for him. We often like to know the end before getting started. Trusting God means no spoilers. We must admit we can't know and control everything. Not holding back can feel risky, so many guys quit too early, thinking God won't notice they're holding back.

What are some ways we might hold back from total obedience to God?

What would it look like for you to go all in with God in a particular area of your life? List three specific details you would need to adjust, let go of, or adopt. Then pause and ask God to help you make these changes.

1.

2.

3.

Young men, the promises of God are true, but rarely do God's promises arrive apart from your participation. The level of your participation affects the experience of the promise (remember Joash's arrows).

We all face challenges and problems that are too big for us on our own. Whatever you might be facing right now is real and might seem overwhelming. It could be a school situation, a family situation, or a "right or wrong" situation. But when God gives you His perspective on what He wants you to do, don't hold back. Don't quit. Don't merge what He says with what your friends say, what you see on social media, or even your own ideas. The answer is already in your hands: complete, total obedience to what He asks you to do. Too many guys are making too many excuses for why they can't lead well, love well, or serve well. God wants you to walk in the power of the promises He has given you.

What has God called you to do that's bigger than you?

In what way does God want you to approach and overcome the obstacles that keep you from obeying?

God won't force victory on you. You have to choose to obey. And you can win through the power of the Holy Spirit inside you, based on what God has revealed to you through His Word and through the confirmation from the Spirit. That is, unless you're satisfied with living in defeat or with only partial victories.

Few guys lay claim to their victory, because few have wholeheartedly embraced God's promises. Few step forward in faith. Far too many would rather make excuses.

What kind of pursuits do we mistake for real purpose? How do those lead us to hold back from pursuing God's purpose for our lives?

We run on empty when we hold back from giving our best to God. Pursuing success though position, power, and possessions often camouflages a misguided purpose. But position, power, and possessions don't last. What lasts is what's done in obedience to the King of kings and the Ruler over all.

What do you need to let go of to walk in faith?

PRAY

Pray for the courage you need to let go of everything that holds you back from fully experiencing the victories that are yours in Jesus Christ. Ask God to reveal to you anything that stands between you and those victories. Give Him praise ahead of time for what He's about to do in your life.

NO MORE EXCUSES

BE THE MAN GOD MADE YOU TO BE!

TONY EVANS

SESSION 3
NO MORE WEAK LEADERSHIP

START

Last week we recognized the value of embracing leadership and faithfully living out our responsibilities as young men.

In what area did you feel convicted to live with more responsibility?

The Monday after an NFL season ends is known as "Black Monday." The reason is because many coaches lose their jobs on that day. They don't get fired because they dropped a pass or missed a field goal. The coaches get fired because the players under their leadership didn't perform in a way that met the expectations of the team owner. Black Monday in the NFL proves a valuable lesson: Leadership stretches far beyond you.

In what ways are leaders accountable for the people under their care and supervision?

How have you seen leadership modeled by the men in your life? Your father? Your family? Your pastors? Your teachers? Your coaches?

In this week's study we'll explore God's design for a man's leadership. This study calls young men to understand their responsibility as they grow older. While they are not yet ready for the weight of marriage and fatherhood, it's never too early to prepare their hearts and minds for who God is calling them to be once they reach those places in life. You can't expect a boy to become a man overnight; they must be trained along the way. God has a definite design in mind for strong leaders, and He has created men to live out that design with faithfulness.

Ask someone to pray before watching the video teaching.

WATCH

NOTE: In this video Dr. Evans does a great job helping men understand the balance of their responsibility as leaders. A man's role is to sacrificially lead like Christ, not as a ruler with an iron fist.

Fill in the blanks to follow along as you watch video Session 3.

Since God is the manufacturer, He should be the One who _____ what a man is and who a man truly is to be.

At the core of a _____ of a man and his leadership _____ is that he is responsible, even if he's not to blame.

God created man before he _____ woman because man was to be the _____ not only for the family but for the culture.

> I searched for a man among them who would build up
> a wall and stand in the gap before Me for the land, so
> that I would not destroy it; but I found no one.
> EZEKIEL 22:30

It's possible to be a male by gender but not a man by responsibility, _____, and function.

If you're going to be a real_____, you have to accept accountability to be under_____.

MAN UP

Use the following questions to discuss the video teaching.

Read the following verse together.

> I want you to understand that Christ is the
> head of every man, and the man is the head
> of a woman, and God is the head of Christ.
> 1 CORINTHIANS 11:3

This verse describes a chain of command. As a teenager, you are not in a place to exercise spiritual authority over a woman as this verse describes, but you have chains of command in your life that you can understand. You have to allow Christ to have power and authority in your life before you'll ever experience His peace. You have to respect and honor the authorities in your life—your parents, family, pastors, teachers, coaches—before you can expect anyone to submit to you. It all starts with submitting to the Lordship of Christ in your life first.

What does submitting to Christ look like in practical, everyday actions?

When you build a house, you start by laying the foundation. Everything else that's built on top of it is impacted by the strength and stability of the foundation. If the foundation shifts, cracks will appear on the walls. If the foundation crumbles, the result might be broken pipes or even the collapse of the entire structure. The foundation determines the strength of all that rests on top.

God created men to serve as the foundation of their homes, churches, and communities. This is the future God has planned for you. Strong leadership by men provides stability for others. Weak, fractured leadership leads to broken lives all around. Strong leaders model the leadership of Christ, who laid down His life to serve the church (see Mark 10:45; Eph. 5:25). Strong leaders seek the benefit of all under their care. That's a foundation you can trust now as a teenager and you can strive to model as you grow into manhood.

Describe some ways you can live as a strong leader in your home, church, school, and community.

In the video Dr. Evans said, "It's possible to be a male by gender but not a man by responsibility, leadership, and function." One way Satan seeks to disarm the advancement of God's kingdom agenda on earth is to downplay the need for male leadership. But strong male leadership is essential to carrying out God's rule.

How have you experienced someone who is male by gender but not a man by responsibility, leadership, and function?

When Adam hid from God in the garden and sought to cover himself with leaves, he was using gifts from God to hide behind. After all, God had provided the plants Adam used to cover himself. We do the same thing today. Although the gifts we hide behind might not be clothes made from leaves, they might include our personality, our intelligence, our athletic skills, or our God-given blessings. Using our gifts and blessings to advance God's kingdom fulfills the calling of a young kingdom man. But hiding behind them to say, "Hey, I'm not so bad after all," as Adam did, is an effort to avoid taking responsibility. Rather than hide, I want to encourage you to rise to the calling of strong leadership that God has given to you. The past no longer controls you. You can lead well—in your churches, schools, families, and friendships—starting today.

In what ways might guys attempt to hide behind their blessings to give the outward appearance that they're strong spiritual leaders?

What specific, practical steps can you take this week to grow toward God's standard of leadership for you?

PRAYER

Close the session with prayer.

Father, You've charged me with the calling of leadership.
As a young man under Your kingdom rule and authority, I accept
that call in every area of my life, starting with my own heart and
will. Give me wisdom and insight to regularly and consistently live
as the leader You've created me to be. In Christ's name, amen.

DAY 1
HIT THE STREETS

OVERCOMING NEGATIVE OUTCOMES

Negative outcomes always occur when a person sins. The Bible affirms this truth in Adam's story. Scripture calls the outcome death. Sin and death are always linked. You can't sin and not expect to die. Sin also causes separation in some form. This separation may be spiritual, emotional, or relational. Paul wrote:

> Therefore, just as sin entered the world through one man, and death through sin, in this way death spread to all people, because all sinned.
> ROMANS 5:12 (CSB)

You can overcome the negative outcomes of sin by applying the truth of God's Word to each form of death.

I. SPIRITUAL SEPARATION

A spiritual rift forms in your relationship with God when you sin. However, good news comes through the death, burial, and resurrection of Jesus Christ. Through Christ your relationship with God can be restored to a deep level of intimacy. But first you must confess your sins and repent. Even if you are already a Christian, you must be in the habit of confession and turning away from sin in your life:

> If we confess our sins, He is faithful and righteous to forgive us our sins and to cleanse us from all unrighteousness.
> 1 JOHN 1:9

2. EMOTIONAL SEPARATION

Sin also takes an emotional strain on you. Over time the cumulative effect of sin can lead to devastating emotional results, whether through addictions, damaged relationships, or simply emotionally shutting down. However, when you repent of your sins, God can restore your emotional well-being:

> Create in me a clean heart, O God,
> And renew a steadfast spirit within me.
> PSALM 51:10

3. RELATIONAL SEPARATION

Difficulties in your relationships—in your family, school, or your friends—are a direct result of sin. Whether this separation occurs because of your own sins or those of others, forgiving yourself or the person who wronged you will usher in relational healing. Paul reminded us where to begin and, more importantly, why:

> Be kind to one another, tender-hearted, forgiving
> each other, just as God in Christ also has forgiven you.
> EPHESIANS 4:32

Sin brings about negative outcomes, but you can overcome them by applying these Scriptural principles to the spiritual, emotional, and relational spheres of your life.

LACE 'EM UP

Overcome a negative outcome in your life this week! Is there someone you are at odds with? Seek that individual out and ask forgiveness for your part in the falling out. Also, be quick to forgive them for whatever role they played, whether they ask for it or not. Forgive because Jesus forgave you.

DAY 2
SHAME ON YOU

"Shame on you" is a common phrase parents tell their children in an effort to correct their behavior. Maybe a teacher said it to you when you were in elementary school. The phrase seeks to let someone know that his behavior doesn't align with the expectations of the authority figure.

Read Genesis 2:25–3:12 and answer the following questions.

What happened between Genesis 2:25 and Genesis 3:10 that caused Adam to feel shame about his nakedness?

In what way does personal sin contribute to our feelings of shame and fear?

Shame causes many people to hide, not only from God but also from themselves and the people they love. Shame leaves its imprint on you at such a deep level that you may feel other people know what you did just by looking at you. It dampens your confidence, destroys your dignity, and silences your speech. Shame is a tool Satan employs to sideline the children of God. All true leadership is rooted in God's leadership, and shame keeps you from embracing His leadership and from drawing near "with confidence to the throne of grace" (Heb. 4:16).

How does this story reveal weakness in Adam's leadership? How can personal shame disrupt our relationships? Why does Satan seek to divide our relationships?

Eve ate the fruit first and then gave it to Adam. He wasn't exercising care over creation as God had commanded him. Notice that God asked Adam where he was, not Eve. This doesn't mean God didn't hold Eve accountable for her actions, but it seems to indicate that God held Adam to a standard of leadership that Adam didn't meet. Adam then blamed both Eve and God for his decision. He blamed God because it was God who gave Eve to Adam and he blamed Eve because she gave him the fruit to eat. Weak leadership always blames others, is born in sin, and often breaks down our personal relationships.

Has shame ever created distance in your relationship with God? If so, in what ways?

As you have probably experienced, many schools have created the option for an online platform for learning, and students no longer go to a school building for the majority of their education. While these online platforms have been a creative solution to many problems our society has faced over the last few years, video calls, texts, virtual classrooms, and email don't allow the opportunity for a greater level of nonverbal feedback and intuitive understanding. Studies indicate that a lot of our communication is nonverbal. Remove that element of closeness, and you remove much of the communication process altogether.

Why do you think Satan came to Adam and Eve when they weren't in God's presence? He knew if he could catch them in a moment when they weren't close to their Creator, he could tempt them and interfere with God's purposes and plans for their lives. Shame puts distance between people and makes meaningful dialogue and deep sharing a struggle rather than a flow.

What should Adam have done instead of hiding from God?

Adam went in the opposite direction of God's presence when he experienced shame. Often, we do the same. If Satan can keep us from walking with God, he can keep much of what God wants to accomplish through us from being done as well.

Sin negatively affects our relationship with God at such a deep level that we can literally start to avoid Him and go into spiritual hiding. Somehow we convince ourselves that if we do, God won't know the things we've done, said, seen, or thought. Strong leadership means we take ownership over our sins and failings and don't allow sin to hinder our relationship with God.

Weak leadership avoids responsibility. Strong leadership humbly admits a mistake and receives forgiveness. How should we approach God when we've sinned?

Be honest with God. Be authentic. Come clean. Throw away the fig leaves. They'll wear out anyhow, and they don't look all that good on you. Shame is a tool of Satan to keep you from living out your full purpose and destiny. It's a clever tool that holds many guys back. But if there were no such thing as sin, there would have been no need for a Savior. Jesus died so that your sin wouldn't enslave you. You're forgiven. You're clean. He paid the price. You don't have to hide and fail to accept responsibility.

Read the following verse.

There is now no condemnation for
those who are in Christ Jesus.
ROMANS 8:1

Are you willing to let your shame go and accept the complete forgiveness Christ offers you?

God knew where to find Adam, and He knows where to find you too. And when He does, He will have three questions for you similar to those He asked Adam:

1. "Where are you?" (Gen. 3:9).
2. "Who told you that you were naked?" (Gen. 3:11).
3. "What is this you have done?" (Gen. 3:13).

God is asking you these questions so that you can answer them, not because He doesn't know the answers. He wants to see whether you're going to tell Him and yourself the truth. He doesn't want to hear you say you made a mistake or had a temporary lapse in judgment. It's deeper than that. Sinful rebellion against a holy God brings consequences. Repentance must come with an honest acknowledgment of what you've done.

All of the issues and crises we face today because of sin in the world have nothing to do with fruit. They have to do with what the fruit stood for, what it meant. Eating the fruit declared that Adam and Eve wanted to be like God. They wanted to be their own gods. The defining issue was whether they wanted to surrender to God or make their own decisions. Because they chose to exalt themselves above God's rule and reign in their lives, they broke fellowship with God. The natural outgrowth of their sin caused them to hide and separate themselves from the intimacy they once knew.

List some ways God wants to free you from the shame of your past and set you free to walk the path of leadership He has for you.

PRAY

Pray about your willingness to come clean with God.
Ask Him to remove any stain of shame that may still linger
in your life. Praise Him that in Christ you're fully forgiven
and can access His authority and rule with all the boldness
and courage that comes from a relationship with Him.

DAY 3
IT JUST KEEPS GOING AND GOING AND GOING

You may have seen a commercial featuring the Energizer Bunny. This pink toy has spent decades advertising the power of the Energizer brand of batteries. The message is that if you use Energizer batteries, the devices in which they're placed will have enough power to last longer than other batteries. They'll just keep going and going and going. It's a cute and sometimes annoying ad, but it definitely gets its point across.

Guys, your impact as a leader has the potential to keep going and going and going as well. Whether that impact is good or bad, the repercussions will last longer than you might imagine. In Exodus, God tells us that the consequences for wrong choices can be passed from generation to generation:

> You shall not worship [idols] or serve them; for I, the LORD your God, am a jealous God, visiting the iniquity of the fathers on the children, on the third and the fourth generations of those who hate Me, but showing lovingkindness to thousands, to those who love Me and keep My commandments.
> EXODUS 20:5-6

Notice that God also said He will give blessings to thousands as well. What you do reaches far beyond just you. Think about all the places your decisions have an impact:

- School
- Your Future
- Friends
- Family (current and future)
- Community
- Church

That's just to name a few of the people and groups you can influence. It's a wakeup call, isn't it? It wouldn't be so bad if our mistakes only affected us. But our mistakes can be passed on and on to many succeeding generations. They also affect the people where we go to school, the church where we worship, and our neighborhood and communities.

Of course, the principle works the other way too. Our faithfulness can bless others for generations to come. It's no wonder Satan targets men. He understands how legacy works. He knows the damage he can do if he can produce legacies of destruction rather than legacies of faithfulness.

Read the following verse.

> One generation will praise Your works to another,
> And will declare Your mighty acts.
> PSALM 145:4

What must happen first in your heart for you to declare God's mighty acts to others?

When has a decision someone else made caused you problems?

When has a decision someone else made been a blessing to you?

We must open ourselves up to be the men, now and in the future, that God can perform mighty acts through. Sometimes we're content to look back on something God did through us in the past and rest on that accomplishment, as if that's all God ever wants to do through us. If we want to be used by God, we have to make ourselves available to Him constantly. God is in the business of working regularly in our lives.

Why is it important to not just rest on God's past work in your heart?

The truth is, you are more likely to be faithful to God when you see others (especially men) live out their faith as evidence of its reality in their lives. When you see people who aren't faithful, it is probably a discouragement to your faith. Many younger people turn away from God because they don't see authenticity in people who claim to follow Jesus. Don't contribute to this statistic. Be faithful to live out and proclaim God's mighty acts in your life as you grow into manhood.

When was the most recent time you had a conversation with someone else about what God is doing in your life?

Why is it important to demonstrate an authentic relationship with God to the people we are around?

Think about this domino-effect; to our forefathers, faith was an experience. To the next generation after them, faith was their inheritance. Then, for the next generation, faith became a convenience. Now, for many in your generation, faith is a nuisance. Why? Because many men have failed to model faith as the living, growing, and powerful relationship with God it's meant to be. Many men have failed to demonstrate a genuine level of discipline or commitment to Jesus in their lives.

A disciplined commitment to faith means sticking to it and avoiding diversions that will distract you from making a kingdom impact at school, in your church, and in your family. George Allen was the coach of the Washington Football Team in the early 1970s (then called the Redskins). He was often invited to the White House for dinner during the season, but would turn President Nixon down.[1] He didn't want anything to distract him from his task, not even the president. Allen had no objection to dining at the White House, but the timing would have undermined his priorities. We have to turn things down, even good things, if they don't align with our priority to follow Christ with our whole life.

What are some actions you can take to guide those around you to a greater level of faith?

Describe the difference in importance between talking about your faith and modeling a life of faith for those around you.

Young men, it's never too early to think about the legacy you will leave behind. After you graduate, what will people say about you? How will you be remembered? Invest in what will last for eternity. Spend your time strengthening your own faith and others in their faith. A legacy of faith lasts throughout eternity.

PRAY

Pray that God will reveal to you more areas of impact than you're currently aware of. Ask Him to show you ways you can begin investing in a legacy as a young kingdom man. Pray about ways you're influencing your friends. Ask God to give you grace to lead and love others greater than you thought possible.

NO MORE EXCUSES

BE THE MAN GOD MADE YOU TO BE!

TONY EVANS

SESSION 4
NO MORE GOING THROUGH THE MOTIONS

START

Welcome to Session 4 of *No More Excuses*.

Last week we considered an issue that's all too common: weak leadership.

Weak leadership has effects that extend beyond us. What's one area you've felt led to step up and lead better?

No boxing champion attained that status by simply going through the motions. No Olympic gold medalist reached that pinnacle of achievement through a ho-hum attitude or routine. No band ever got great without rehearsing or practicing their instruments. Settling into predictability gets us stuck in a dangerous location: the comfort zone. Nothing amazing ever came from a comfort zone.

In what ways are you tempted to just go through the motions?

How does going through the motions contribute to a life of mediocrity?

Meaning is found beyond simply going through the motions. It comes when you commit to a sold-out, all-in, no-turning-back pursuit of God Himself. He's ready. Are you? Let's look together at Solomon's quest for meaning and learn how it relates to you today.

Ask someone to pray before watching the video teaching.

WATCH

NOTE: Help the young men in your group watch this teaching and feel challenged to begin to lay a groundwork for habits and attitudes that will guide their hearts and minds as they grow into manhood.

Fill in the blanks to follow along as you watch video Session 4.

Far too many men are living without _____ in their lives.

When a man disconnects from _____, he's disconnected from the _____ of meaning.

If all of life is only in this _____, you'll never have the life that you're looking for. You'll just go through the _____.

God will _____ meaninglessness in the life of a man who does things _____ Him being connected to it.

Make God your _____, and He will inject _____ in your life because He will make eternity enter time.

MAN UP

Use the following questions to discuss the video teaching.

Read the following verse together.

The conclusion, when all has been heard, is: fear God and
keep His commandments, because this applies to every person.
ECCLESIASTES 12:13

Solomon had it all. Status. Power. Fame. Money. Women. Freedom. Attention. Control. You name it; he had it. You'd think he would have been the happiest man on earth, but he wasn't. In fact, the man who had it all spent a lot of his time pondering the meaning of life. He wanted to figure out why he was here and what he should do.

Neither Solomon's pursuits nor his conquests gave him the kind of satisfaction that lasted. Like when you take that last delicious bite of steak, he wanted more. He wanted authentic meaning, the kind that doesn't depend on other people's validation, a paycheck, or a competition to win.

In what ways does Solomon's pursuit of significance and meaning mirror the quests of many guys today?

How can a lack of meaning contribute to a lifestyle of just going through the motions?

Going through the motions creates a life that looks like life but without deeper meaning. It takes our responsibilities at school, to our friends, families, at home, and to God and makes them nothing more than a routine. It saps all meaning and purpose from our lives.

Because we've been created in the image of God, we are born with a need for meaning, creativity, significance, and purpose. We mirror God's greatness within us, so a life in which we just go through the motions wears us out, not only physically but also emotionally, spiritually, and psychologically.

Brainstorm some creative ways to break out of the box of going through the motions. Begin with your spiritual life then move outward.

Many guys today are busy doing stuff like hanging out with friends, going to school, playing sports, playing video games, and preparing for the future. They are looking toward these activities to give them meaning in life. It's not God's desire that we find our ultimate meaning in what we are doing. Ultimate meaning is only found in God because God is the source of all meaning.

What are some common places guys look for meaning other than God?

Read James 4:13-16. God supplies meaning in your life because He is the supplier of life itself. Nothing exists outside of Him. The primary principle in identifying your purpose and, as a result, identifying your meaning involves locating God. Don't search for yourself, your purpose, or your significance. Search for God. He knows where those goals all end.

Have you seen someone make plans, only to have God intervene and suddenly change them? What did they learn?

Solomon arrived at this conclusion when all was said and done: "Fear God and keep His commandments" (Eccl. 12:13). Another way to say it is, "align your thoughts, words, and actions underneath the overarching rule of God in every area of your life." That's God's kingdom agenda for you. When you do that, you'll experience the visible expression of His power and purpose both in and through you.

Identify one specific way you can align your thoughts, words, or actions this week underneath God's overarching rule.

PRAYER

Close the session with prayer.

Father, mold us into young men of meaning and significance.
Give us wisdom to avoid wasting our lives and instead to pursue
You and Your purposes. Help us break out of our comfort zones
of going through the motions and discover lives of significance
as You work in and through us. In Christ's name, amen.

DAY 1
HIT THE STREETS

THREE STEPS TO SUCCESS

If you want to find the secret to life and success, look to the Author of life. In other words, if you want to find your purpose, don't go looking for your purpose. Look for the purpose giver. The clearest way to find out who you are isn't to look at the guy in the mirror but to look at God, the One who gives you your identity. When you find your Creator, you find you. God has given us three clear steps we can follow to live a life of success.

1. FEAR GOD

To fear God isn't the kind of fear you might get if you watch a scary movie or when you walk into the cafeteria on your first day at a new school. The fear of God involves reverence and honor. It's similar to the fear you have for a judge in a courtroom or when you walk into the principal's office. When you fear God, it shows up in your thoughts and actions. When you seek to align what you do and who you are with Him, His Word, and His will for your life, you're living a life that fears God.

2. KEEP HIS COMMANDMENTS

God has revealed a number of commandments throughout Scripture, but Jesus gave us the perfect summary for them all: love God and love others.

> He said to him, "Love the Lord your God with all your heart, with all your soul, and with all your mind. This is the greatest and most important command. The second is like it: Love your neighbor as yourself."
> MATTHEW 22:37-39 (CSB)

When you obey these two commandments completely, you'll naturally live out all of the other commandments. Love is compassionately and righteously pursuing the well-being of another person. It isn't primarily an emotion. Love is an action. Make loving God and others your highest commitment in life and you'll be spiritually successful in what you do.

3. INCLUDE GOD IN YOUR PLANNING

Planning is good and important, but excluding God from your planning is a sure way to head in the wrong direction. James boldly wrote:

> Come now, you who say, "Today or tomorrow we will go to such and such a city, and spend a year there and engage in business and make a profit." Yet you do not know what your life will be like tomorrow. You are just a vapor that appears for a little while and then vanishes away. Instead, you ought to say, "If the Lord wills, we will live and also do this or that." But as it is, you boast in your arrogance; all such boasting is evil.
> JAMES 4:13-16

Including God in your planning means allowing His perspective and Word to have an impact on all you do. It also leaves room for the Holy Spirit to change your mind, opinions, and plans midstream.

Fearing God, keeping His commandments, and including Him in your planning are three critical components for becoming the young man God is designing you to be. God created you to be great and to fulfill your destiny. By following His road map, you'll discover a life of purpose and fulfillment you never dreamed possible.

LACE 'EM UP

Let's think about the future. Right now, what are your plans for your life? Have you allowed God to impact your plans? What needs to happen to allow Him to take control of your plans for your future?

On another sheet of paper or in a journal, write out the answers to these questions. Prayerfully think about them and ask God to guide you as you ponder how to be successful in His eyes as you move into the future.

DAY 2
CHASING THE WIND

Have you ever been on a cruise? When you stand on the boat and look out over the vast ocean, you recognize just how small you really are. You are surrounded by water in every direction. You come to see that you are a little speck on a seemingly huge boat that is itself a dot in the middle of a gigantic ocean.

When you go to the rear of the boat, you'll noticed a striking phenomenon. As the ship sails through the ocean, it's mass creates a huge disturbance in the water. But as the choppy water moves away from the boat, it smooths out again and everything goes back to normal. The ship ultimately leaves no permanent mark on the ocean.

Many years from now, at the end of your life, what type of impact do you hope to have had on the world?

What steps are you taking to ensure that's the legacy you're leaving?

Legacy is an important subject on my mind right now. Even as young men, it should be on your mind. Too many of us go through our lives and leave little or no impact for good. Even King Solomon wrestled with this fear. Having a purpose and making an impact for God's kingdom matters. But how do we do that according to God's kingdom plan?

Read Ecclesiastes 1:12-15 and answer the following questions.

What's the "grievous task" (v. 13) Solomon referred to in this passage?

Describe the result of "striving after wind" (v. 14). How does this illustration apply to a life lived outside of God's plan?

Do you ever struggle with your own meaning or purpose? If so, how does that struggle affect your emotions or productivity?

What does chasing the wind look like in your life? How closely is the struggle for meaning and purpose tied to chasing the wind?

If you've ever tried to catch wind, you know it's uncatchable. Not only are we blind to its movement, but we also can't touch it. It's impossible to catch something you can't see or touch (other than a cold). Yet that's exactly what King Solomon compared life on earth to. Life lived apart from God's divine wisdom and plan amounts to nothing more than the futile pursuit of "striving after wind" (v. 14).

We start to chase the wind when we go through life without giving thought to our eternal purpose or to God's leadership in our lives. When that happens, other goals replace the goal of knowing and living for Him, and we chase a life that truly isn't worth having.

What are the things that guys chase after that they think will give their lives meaning?

King Solomon, who had it all, said his life was meaningless apart from God's rule and authority. Why do you think God's rule and authority play such a critical role in our own pursuit of significance and satisfaction in life?

God has put within each one of us a sense of the eternal, a longing for things beyond space and time. He has given us desires to have ultimate purpose and meaning. Although God has placed us in the routine of earthly life (v. 13), He wants us to look beyond the realm of earth for something greater.

Read Ecclesiastes 3:11. When have you felt the pull of eternity in your soul? How might this longing motivate you to live a life that goes beyond simply checking off tasks and going through the motions?

You can't find your ultimate purpose in life by looking at life on this earth. The only way you can find the answer to the eternal question of purpose, significance, and meaning that echoes loudly in your heart is by looking into eternity's definition of these things. And when you looks into eternity's perspective, you'll find God's answer waiting for you.

The minute you start looking at life to find the meaning of life, you miss the very life you're looking for. As long as you focus on money, power, pleasure, achievement, relationships, or anything else to find the meaning of life, you've lost what you're looking for.

Why can we not find life when we look at life itself for the answers?

Why is it important to focus only on God and His view of your significance and meaning?

As young men, you often seek to find your significance and meaning in achieving success at school, on the athletic field, in relationships, or even in conquering video games. Although many of these are good things from a God who loves us, if we don't pursue things with God's eternal purpose in mind, we're simply going through the motions. We'll fall short of the life that God has for us.

Only when you view life as God's gift can you begin to find its purpose. Only when you live with an eternal perspective can you find life's meaning. In other words, if you want to find your purpose, don't go looking for your purpose. Look for the purpose giver. If you want to find the secret to life, look to the Author of life. When you find your Creator, you find you.

Jesus said:

> I came that they may have life, and have it abundantly.
> JOHN 10:10

Life isn't found in the living but in the Living One. Jesus agreed with Solomon. Life is a gift from God, and He defines it for you.

In what ways are you merely going through the motions?

God often uses our past experiences, as well as our gifts, passions, and opportunities, to lead us to our ultimate purpose in Him. Consider those aspects of your life. How could you continue to pursue these same passions in ways that bring ultimate honor and glory to God?

PRAY

Pray about aligning all of your life underneath God's overarching, comprehensive rule. Ask God to reveal more answers to the previous questions and to fine-tune your understanding of His purpose for you. Seek to obey Him by reading, meditating on, and studying His Word. Praise Him for the purpose He created you to fulfill.

DAY 3
GET TO WORK

Dr. Kenneth Cooper uses every opportunity he can to present the gospel. In the world of doctors, he's pretty famous, being credited as the founder of aerobic exercise. Dr. Cooper has always believed in pursuing great health. "But Tony," he says when Dr. Evans goes in for his regular checkups, "this is just a platform I use to introduce people to God." Dr. Cooper has found his calling in his work. Many people do. Maybe you just see the things you're doing at this stage in life—school, band, sports, chores—simply as an obligation to fulfill and not something you're always excited about. You can still do more than simply go through the motions when you dedicate your efforts to the Lord.

Solomon told us that finding satisfaction in our activities is a gift from God Himself. And Paul reminded us that whatever we do, we're to do it for the glory of God.

Read the following verses.

> There is nothing better for a man than to eat and drink and tell himself that his labor is good. This also I have seen that it is from the hand of God.
> ECCLESIASTES 2:24

> Whatever you do, do your work heartily, as for the Lord rather than for men, knowing that from the Lord you will receive the reward of the inheritance. It is the Lord Christ whom you serve.
> COLOSSIANS 3:23-24

How can knowing that the things you do are gifts from God and that He is the One you serve help you escape the rut of going through the motions in your life?

Describe the difference between going through the motions with your school work, chores, or practicing your sport or instrument versus fully engaging in the activities of your life.

God can give you the ability to enjoy these things. That process starts with your relationship with Him, but it should extend to the environment where you expend your effort. God wants you to do things you enjoy doing and can do well for His glory.

You may not be thrilled that this stage in your life is dominated by education and adults telling you what to do. But these things are preparing you for the rest of your life. It might not be your favorite thing to hear, but your perspective is narrow right now.

The goal of your life isn't to make good grades, be named the team captain or first chair, or even to stack your resume to set you up for a bright future. The ultimate goal of everything you are doing right now is to make a lasting impact for God and His kingdom. Remember the story of Dr. Cooper? Remember his words? "This is just a platform I use to introduce people to God."

What are some ways you can participate in the activities of your life so that God receives the ultimate glory? Who is someone that does this well?

Once a close family member of Dr. Evans had to undergo surgery, and the family gathered at the hospital prior to the procedure. When the doctors and nurses came in to consult with her about the surgery, they did more than that. They called all of the family members around and made it clear they do their work for the Lord. Though the knife would be in the surgeon's hand, it was God who guided it. Though medication could provide healing or prevent infection, it was God who granted these results. Then they openly prayed with everyone, inviting God into the surgery room so that His presence and wisdom would be present during the procedure.

Each of us can see our activities in life with an eternal perspective. The person in the desk next to you isn't just a fellow student but someone made in the image of God with an eternal soul. If they don't know Jesus, you have the opportunity to introduce them to Him through your words and actions. Beyond that, we can serve one another sacrificially by lending a hand or offering an encouraging word. When we start to believe God placed us where we are, it changes our perspective.

How does our fear of what people think or what they might say keep us from boldly proclaiming God's name to others?

When you understand that God alone is your source and that everyone and everything else is a resource, you won't give in to fear or remain quiet about His name.

Why is it important to understand that God is your source?

In what ways does knowing this spiritual truth free you to do all God has called you to do?

Living as a testimony to Christ doesn't have to be thumping your Bible or harassing people about Jesus. You can model integrity and set yourself apart as Daniel did when he lived and worked in the pagan kingdom of Babylon.

Super Bowl-winning coach Tony Dungy, a friend Dr. Evans, had the rare opportunity to play on what's arguably the best defense in the NFL during the height of its dominance—the Pittsburgh Steelers in the 1970s. The Steel Curtain, as it was known, was great. But Dungy recently shared one of the secrets of the team's success.

He said most people thought the Steelers' defensive players were great because they were so committed to football and to winning. Although they were, Dungy revealed that they had a commitment even higher than that. They were committed to working for the Lord. To them, playing football was their job. Winning games was their job. This strong work ethic showed up in all they did because they believed and publicly proclaimed in the locker room that to give all their effort was the way to serve God. God expected nothing less than their best.

Dungy said most of the players showed up early for practice and stayed late, and they encouraged others to do the same. The reward of their work resulted in four Super Bowl championships in one decade. But their eternal rewards, which are far greater, will be awaiting them as well.

Working hard and being all you can be are part of God's design for you. God Himself worked in establishing His creation and maintaining it. Similarly, Jesus spent His whole earthly life working. We can assume He worked hard in Joseph's carpenter shop, and He spent His entire ministry working out the will of His Father. On the cross He stated that His work was finished (see John 19:30).

Young men, simply going through the motions in life wastes your God-given opportunities to do things in a way that brings God all the glory. Because you're serving God and not yourself, you have good reason to work hard and to the best of your ability. Whatever you're doing, big or small, do it with all your heart and as unto the Lord (see Eph. 6:7). He will see your effort and will bless you.

Read Ephesians 6:7. What changes in you when you see the Lord as your ultimate boss?

What's one concrete step you can take to be more fully engaged in whatever it is that you do in the hopes that your friends and those around you will see your good work and give glory to your Father in heaven?

PRAY

Pray and commit your activities to the Lord. Proverbs 16:3 says if you commit your work to the Lord, "your plans will be established." Every day when you wake up, say a prayer asking God to use you at school, at home, at practice, or wherever you find yourself for His kingdom purposes.

NO MORE EXCUSES

BE THE MAN GOD MADE YOU TO BE!

TONY EVANS

SESSION 5

NO MORE COMPROMISING YOUR INTEGRITY

START

Welcome to Session 5 of *No More Excuses.*

Last week we examined the dangers of going through the motions.

Why is going through the motions such an easy pattern to fall into if we're not careful?

True integrity defines who we are when no one can see us. It involves words we say and actions we do in private or even when we're with our closest, most trusted set of friends. Words said behind closed doors or in a locker room often reveal who we really are far more clearly than words said in public.

What actions come to mind when you hear that a guy has compromised his integrity?

Why is maintaining your integrity so important?

We may think we can hide who we really are in secret, but God sees. God knows. And often in His providential ways, other people come to find out as well. Just ask all the high-profile athletes, celebrities, politicians, and even pastors who have lost their jobs in the past few years over something they said or did in private. In contrast, true integrity doesn't shift based on the people present or on the location. True integrity stays consistent throughout each moment of our lives.

Ask someone to pray before watching the video teaching.

WATCH

NOTE: The key statement in this session is the final quote below, "God is calling us to integrity now." Remind guys that if they decide to wait until they are grown to start living with integrity, it will be difficult to break the bad habits they began when they were younger. It's best to start off right and live with integrity today.

Fill in the blanks to follow along as you watch video Session 5.

Integrity: Living up to one's legitimate standards

It is when men decide that God will set the _____ and it is that _____ they will pursue that we become men of integrity.

Keep the standard and you _____ up to meet it at it's intended height.

We want God to show up with our lack of _____, but God shows up when we demonstrate _____.

Sometimes when you _____ integrity as a man, it will cost you.

"Daniel, servant of the living God, has your God, whom you constantly serve, been able to deliver you from the lions?"
DANIEL 6:20

You will find _____, as a man, in the lions' den, and God _____ you to keep the standard.

"God is calling us to integrity now."

MAN UP

Use the following questions to discuss the video teaching.

Read the following verse together.

> Now when Daniel knew that the document was signed, he
> entered his house (now in his roof chamber he had windows
> open toward Jerusalem); and he continued kneeling on
> his knees three times a day, praying and giving thanks
> before his God, as he had been doing previously.
> DANIEL 6:10

As a child, you probably heard the story of Daniel in the lion's den. We often focus on the lions and their refusal to eat Daniel for dinner. Yet an important principle in this story is often overshadowed by the sensational aspect of God's power over lions—the principle of Daniel's consistent integrity.

Why do you think Daniel left his windows open when he prayed instead of protecting himself and closing them?

Describe some ways guys may seek to rationalize our way out of complete obedience to God in the face of risk.

The largest, most dangerous group of animals in Africa are known as the big five—the lion, leopard, buffalo, elephant, and rhino. Though these big animals are amazing, the continent also has tons of other amazing animals that are just as interesting and just as dangerous. A lot of guys look at sin the same way, thinking, "If I just stay away from the big ones I'll be fine." The "big ones" might be terrible, but the "little ones" are just as deadly. God desires for us to walk in integrity in things great and small, because in reality, there is not such thing as a small sin.

What do most teen guys consider "big" sins? Why are the "small" sins just as deadly?

In the video Dr. Evans said, "What far too many of us as men are doing is we're lowering the standard—dunking at a lower standard and thinking we've done something. Rather than keeping God's standard high and saying we've got to raise ourselves to meet His standard, we've allowed the world to dumb down God's standard. Therefore, we have dumbed down our integrity."

What are some ways we've dumbed down God's standard?

What is an example of us lowering the goal, dunking on it, and thinking we've done something great?

Daniel could pray with the window open because he believed God was his source. God owned the outcome. Young men, God is your source. Your youth isn't your source. Your intelligence isn't. Even your family isn't. Your family's money isn't. Although we may have the ability to make choices in life, no one has the final say but God.

How can believing God is your source free you to make decisions rooted in biblical integrity?

God has a standard of integrity. It isn't hidden from us but revealed to us in His Word. We're all called to love God and demonstrate His love to others. This is the basis of all ethical living in God's kingdom. His standard encompasses all of life. If you haven't lived up to this standard in the past, you can start today. Start now. Never let fear dictate your decisions. God has your back when you align your life under His standard.

What's one practical action you can take this week to align yourself more fully with God's standard of biblical integrity? It could be something you do at school, at home, or in your personal spiritual development. Commit to hold one another accountable for this action at the next group session.

PRAYER

Close the session with prayer.

Father, in a culture that consistently lowers standards, we want to remain focused on You. We want to aim high in all we do, knowing we serve an audience of one. Convict us when our integrity needs to improve. Forgive us when we've failed You in the past. Strengthen us to live according to Your standard. In Christ's name, amen.

DAY 1
HIT THE STREETS

HOW TO INTERNALIZE INTEGRITY

Living a life of integrity includes all areas of your life. Your public integrity is what other people see at school or in your home and church. Your private integrity exists between you and God, applying to what you say and do when no one else will find out. Keeping your integrity level high is God's standard for you. Blessings will come as a result of your personal integrity, just as Daniel experienced protection from the lions when thrown into their den.

Here are five ways you can cultivate integrity.

1. DON'T WAIT AROUND

Don't wait for your parents to tell you, your friends to do it too, or even for your circumstances to improve before you make a change toward integrity in your heart. Integrity refers to who you are on the inside, regardless of what's happening on the outside. Don't blame others if your level of integrity isn't where it should be.

2. SET YOUR STANDARDS IN ADVANCE

Decide on the standards you won't compromise before you find yourself in the middle of a problem. You can't become a man of integrity on the spot. You can't wait until the action gets hot and heavy to make decisions of integrity. Establish biblical guidelines for integrity in advance.

3. DEVELOP A CONSISTENT DEVOTIONAL LIFE

Make spending time with God the rule, not the exception. As you see in Daniel's case, cultivating your walk with God throughout the day will do more than anything else in helping you become a man of integrity.

4. FIND FRIENDS WHO WILL HOLD YOU ACCOUNTABLE

Find friends who ask hard questions about what you're doing and not doing. Be authentic. Cultivate trust in the relationship that allows you to share failures. Don't judge, and you won't be judged (see Luke 6:37). Stay in contact and reach out when you need a reminder to stay strong. If a group like this isn't available in your life, begin praying now that God would send guys into your life to help hold you accountable and for you to hold them accountable as well.

5. FOCUS ON GOD, NOT YOUR CIRCUMSTANCES

If Daniel had focused on his circumstances, he would have become overwhelmed with fear. If he had dwelled only on how bad things were and what could happen, he would have compromised just like everybody else. If he had focused only on how hard his life was, he could have lost his integrity. He wouldn't have been extraordinary. God didn't save you so that you could become like everybody else. He saved you to be extraordinary.

LACE 'EM UP

Let's live with integrity this week! For one hour keep a thought journal. When a thought passes through your mind that doesn't honor God, mark a tally in the journal. Then, after one hour see how many marks you have.

After that—and this is the most important part—spend time in prayer, asking God to help you live with integrity and for those thoughts to no longer be a part of your thinking.

DAY 2
WALK SECURELY

Integrity is a critical issue today. In a society where people feel they can't trust anyone anymore, integrity is the key to reversing that trend. It's important when you call someone a friend that you can trust him. It's critical for finding mentors you can follow. And it's vital for setting an example for other, younger guys to see in you.

When we talk about integrity, we're talking about a person's trustworthiness. It means what you say and what you mean are the same thing. It means when you make a promise, you keep it. It means when you say you'll do something, you do it.

Read the following verse and answer the questions.

He who walks in integrity walks securely,
But he who perverts his ways will be found out.
PROVERBS 10:9

What does it mean to walk securely?

This verse says a lack of integrity "will be found out." Do you believe this? Besides others knowing, how will a lack of integrity be found out?

In Proverbs 10:9 it says, "he who perverts his ways." According to this verse, who is responsible for your way? If your way is "perverted" who's fault is it?

How can knowing you walk securely contribute to your peace of mind?

There are two ways to live—with or without integrity. Our sin always has a way of being revealed. Even if others don't realize our lack of integrity, God does. Nothing is hidden from His sight (see Heb. 4:13). What's more, God sees beyond the surface and into a person's heart. His sight goes beyond our conduct and into our character and motivation. God always knows our lack of integrity. In contrast, guys who've trusted Christ and are committed to living in line with His standard walk securely, knowing they're right with God and others.

What are some ways Satan seeks to trap us so that we'll compromise our integrity?

Most guys have compromised their integrity at some point. It may have been at school when you looked around and made sure no one was watching before you glanced at your neighbor's paper. Or maybe you've turned your phone, computer, or iPad to private-browsing mode and hit a porn site. After all, who would ever know?

Compromise may not involve anything you're doing. It may all be in your mind. Nonetheless, compromise is still at play because integrity has to do with more than your outward behavior. Integrity is about more than conduct; it's about what happens in your heart.

Would you describe yourself as a person who strives for integrity? Would your friends and family agree?

When we talk about integrity, we aren't talking about your reputation. Your reputation is what other people think of you. You can fake your way to a good reputation. Integrity goes beyond that to what you're really like on the inside. It refers to your character.

What you do when no one is watching is who you are. What you do in secret and what you may think you got away with will come out eventually because the spiritual principle in Proverbs 10:9 holds true. That's why honesty and repentance are key. Only those qualities can correct your heart after compromising your integrity.

The word *repentance* means to make a 180-degree turn. It means turning from your sin, trusting in Christ, and accepting the forgiveness He offers. Why is it important to accept God's forgiveness, mercy, and grace when you've failed?

Why are we often reluctant to do this?

Jesus's sacrifice on the cross covers all sins at all levels of consequence and in all ways. Accepting His forgiveness, however, can sometimes be more difficult for some sins than others. Why? Mostly because our culture puts a higher emphasis on some sins than others. As a result, far too many of us fall back into sin because we live under the chains and oppression of unconfessed sin or unreceived forgiveness.

If we're going to live with integrity rather than look for an excuse to take the easy way out, it will boil down to our personal walk with God. It will come down to our ability to trust Christ's forgiveness for all our sins and to walk in the newness of His love. When we're right with God, we're then able to treat others the way He has called us to do.

Read Psalm 119:9-16. What help has God given us to live according to His standard?

Identify great wisdom in this passage for maintaining integrity.

We'll live with integrity only to the degree that we meet God's standard. God hasn't left us on our own. He cares about our integrity and has given us His Word so that we understand what it means to live in a relationship with Him. The more we focus on His Word, hide it in our hearts, and model our lives after the wisdom we find there, the more we'll live in integrity. But even in moments when we're pressed to make a choice that doesn't honor God, He has given us help:

> No temptation has overtaken you except what is common to mankind. And God is faithful; he will not let you be tempted beyond what you can bear. But when you are tempted, he will also provide a way out so that you can endure it.
>
> 1 CORINTHIANS 10:13 (NIV)

When we're tempted, God knows. Thankfully, He has given us a way out. If you know Jesus, He's alive and working in your life through His Holy Spirit. You don't have to give in to temptation or compromise your integrity. He's present with you to help you overcome.

When you're tempted, why is it helpful to realize that you have a way out?

The next time you're tempted to compromise your integrity, what will be your response?

PRAY

Ask God to reveal areas in which you may have compromised your integrity so that you can identify it, repent of it, and live without compromise. Ask Him to show you ways you can encourage other guys to live with integrity. Seek God's forgiveness for hurting anyone as a result of a lapse in your personal integrity.

DAY 3
STAYING STRONG
IN DIFFICULTIES

Your integrity can be severely tested in adversity. If you don't get the grade you want on a test, that occasion lends itself to doing or saying something you shouldn't far more than if you got an A+. Difficulties diminish our resolve and kick-start our human nature to seek a way to cope.

If you want to know the level of your integrity, measure it at a time when circumstances are tough. What you're really like can be clearly measured when your life is falling apart.

Select the terms that best define you when life is toughest.

- ☐ **Patient**
- ☐ **Irritable**
- ☐ **Gracious**
- ☐ **Judgmental**
- ☐ **Trusting**
- ☐ **Fearful**
- ☐ **Affirming**
- ☐ **Destructive**

Young kingdom men must be defined by the fruit of the Spirit, even when life is tough. Otherwise, we aren't living with integrity. In sports there are gracious losers and immature losers. Gracious losers know they can't win every game, and they congratulate the other team for a hard-fought battle. Immature losers internalize the difficulty, blame others, and often fail to grow as a result of the loss. Losses can send them spiraling downward in their personal lives as well as on the court or field.

The fruit of the Spirit reveals the true level of your integrity, especially in the middle of life's toughest losses.

Read the following verses.

The fruit of the Spirit is love, joy, peace, patience, kindness, goodness, faithfulness, gentleness, self-control; against such things there is no law. Now those who belong to Christ Jesus have crucified the flesh with its passions and desires. If we live by the Spirit, let us also walk by the Spirit. Let us not become boastful, challenging one another, envying one another.
GALATIANS 5:22-26

Would you say these traits are evident in your life? How would greater dependence on Christ cultivate any that are lacking?

The fruit of the Spirit are supernatural attributes that followers of Jesus possess as they know Jesus and walk in the Holy Spirit. The word *fruit* in verse 22 is singular, both in English and in the original Greek language. What this means is that every Christian has all nine of these traits because they are filled with the Holy Spirit. There's no picking and choosing when it comes to the fruit of the Spirit. Although all Christians have at least one spiritual gift or different blends of gifts, every Christian should be marked by love, joy, peace, patience, kindness, goodness, faithfulness, gentleness, and self-control. We may not possess all of the fruit of the Spirit in equal parts, and they may be more evident in one person's life over another, but if you know Jesus, these traits are yours and it is your responsibility as a follower of Christ to develop them in your heart and life.

What confidence does it give you to know these traits are yours simply by knowing Jesus?

How does walking with the Spirit and living in Him help you maintain your integrity?

Walking by the Spirit means we embrace the Holy Spirit's leading and work in our lives. It means we trust His guidance above our own. Yet even guys who walk with the Spirit daily sometimes compromise. Maybe it's recently happened to you. Maybe it's going on right now.

You may be thinking as we study integrity, *I've already compromised. My parents don't trust me. My friends don't respect me. My teachers and coaches think I'm not dependable at school. It's too late for me.*

No, it's not! It's never too late with God. Think about men depicted in Scripture. Moses definitely lost his integrity when he killed the Egyptian, but God gave it back to him at the burning bush and called him to lead Israel. David lost his integrity when he had an affair with Bathsheba and had her husband murdered, but he confessed his sin, and God restored him. In fact, God regarded him as "a man after His own heart" (1 Sam. 13:14). These men had their faults, but they also trusted God and exercised genuine sorrow and repented for what they had done. They left their sin behind and embraced God's will for their lives. You can too.

If you've recently compromised your integrity, whose forgiveness do you need to seek after you've sought God's forgiveness?

What can we learn by seeing ways God used fallen and flawed men like Moses and David for His glory even after they sinned?

God is in the restoration business. He can take failure and turn it into a future of hope. He can take a mess and make a miracle. He can take compromise and restore it to commitment. But He won't do it alone. It requires cooperation on your part, a willingness to be restored to a life of integrity. Just as a person who restores a car often has to strip it to the frame before building it back up again, God sometimes strips us to our core before restoring us with the shine of success.

Why is integrity foundational for us if we want to live as young kingdom men? Do you pay as much attention to your integrity as you do to your popularity or grades?

Over the next week review the fruit of the Spirit found in Galatians 5:22-23 and ask God daily to produce the fruit in your life. What effect do you think that exercise will have on your integrity?

Integrity isn't a subject that gets much airplay in our world. For whatever reason, it doesn't trend or get hashtagged as often as many other things. But integrity stands as the foundation of our greatness as guys. Until we return to embracing, encouraging, and fostering a spirit of integrity in ourselves and in others, we'll continue to face the consequences of ongoing compromise. As a result, we'll continue to fail in our pursuit to leave a lasting impact on those around us. Let's be guys who don't make excuses. Let's live in the full realization of all God has created us to be.

PRAY

Pray that God will show you how to be more authentic with other guys and foster integrity in your life and relationships. Ask God to give you wisdom to lead in this revolutionary cultural change, starting right where you are.

NO MORE EXCUSES

BE THE MAN GOD MADE YOU TO BE!

TONY EVANS

SESSION 6
NO MORE SIFTING THROUGH THE RUBBLE

START

Welcome to Session 6 of *No More Excuses*.

Over the past week you came to understand the importance of being a person of integrity. Let's share what we've learned.

Who's a man who models well what it means to live with integrity?
What's one lesson you can put into practice from his life?

This week we'll focus on sifting through the rubble—our response to failure. Michael Jordan once said, "I've missed more than nine thousand shots in my career. I've lost almost three hundred games. Twenty six times I've been trusted to take the game-winning shot and missed. I've failed over and over and over again in my life. And that is why I succeed."[1]

How do you generally respond when you fail at something?

In what ways can failure contribute to greater success in the future?

Our failures, when responded to with the right mindset, can propel us into greater levels of spiritual development and achievement. But far too often we allow our failures to define, confine, and resign us to lives of mediocrity. The fear of failure is one of the biggest reasons we don't take risks when it comes to our faith. But God has something to say about facing our failures head-on, and He shares it with us over breakfast.

Ask someone to pray before watching the video teaching.

WATCH

NOTE: Your guys may or may not have a closet full of regrets at this stage in their lives. Regardless, there is no doubt they've stumbled at some point along the way. Use the teaching Dr. Evans offers in this session to help them understand the amazing nature of God's grace and His willingness to restore us after we've fallen.

Fill in the blanks to follow along as you watch video Session 6.

We are _____ on God, and we are never to be _____ from Him.

God offers that _____ of grace to every man who's willing to recognize their _____, acknowledge their failure, repent of their failure, and return to the One they failed.

God will give you as many _____ as you are willing to take advantage of.

God wants to _____ something new in your life on the space of your _____.

_____ running. Let's _____ rebuilding.

God wants to do _____ with whatever part of your _____ that's left.

God wants to see you _____ what He created you to be.

You've got to be _____ to be picked up by God, because you can't pick yourself up.

MAN UP

Use the following questions to discuss the video teaching.

Read the following verse together.

When they got out on the land, they saw a charcoal
fire already laid and fish placed on it, and bread.
JOHN 21:9

Jesus cooking breakfast—that would have been a sight to see! The Savior of the universe stoking a charcoal fire, blowing on it to ignite the flame, and preparing the fish. This wasn't any ordinary breakfast either. This breakfast had an intentional purpose. The fish—and the miraculous way they were caught—reminded Peter of his call to ministry years earlier: "Follow Me, and I will make you fishers of men" (see Matt. 4:18-20). The charcoal reminded Peter of his failure when he denied Jesus three times (see John 18:18).

How did the charcoal fire remind Peter of his failure? How could it be used as a tool in his redemption?

Describe the lengths God will go to restore someone. How does that effort make you feel about your own ability to be restored?

When a construction company sets out to build a new skyscraper in an established part of a city, it often has to implode the existing structure to make room for the new building. This removal of the past provides the space for a much more modern and useful facility. God isn't afraid to tear down old patterns of thought, behaviors, and habits in a guy in order to make room for His purpose and destiny to thrive in him. God sees the end from the beginning, so He's not scared off by the mess in between (see Isa. 46:9-10).

How does knowing that God sees us from end to beginning help us overcome the failures that happen in the middle?

In the video Dr. Evans said, "God has a purpose for your life. He has a plan for your life, and yes, we messed it up a lot of times, but God knows how to rebuild. He's the ultimate Mr. Fix-It because He can take what looks like nothing and make it something. He can take something that looks like it has no future and give it a future that a man never thought he could have."

How have you witnessed God's rebuilding and restoration in your life or in someone else's life?

Believe it or not, you can visit the exact location where Peter preached his first sermon after Jesus restored him. It's called the Southern Steps in Israel, and there more than three thousand people put their faith in Jesus Christ in response to Peter's message (see Acts 2). Imagine standing where Peter stood that day. It would be a great reminder of God's faithfulness and that He can use us in spite of ourselves. Not all of us have publicly rejected Jesus like Peter did, but each one of us, in our own way, has minimized Jesus either through words or actions at some point in time. Yet Jesus remains faithful to draw us back to Him when we repent.

What are some of the things that hold us back from accepting the call of Jesus to restoration after we've failed?

A false sense of pride and a spirit of self-sufficiency are the surest killers of influence and impact in our lives. Young men, when you've failed, admit it. Acknowledge your sin to God and repent. He's in the business of rebuilding, but it starts with your honesty and sorrow over your sin. Peter went on to do even greater ministry after he was restored than he ever did before. After being restored by Jesus he relied on God's power rather than his own. The lesson of Peter is a lesson for all of us.

How can we create an environment where we feel free to acknowledge our failures, know that we're in a safe place and our dirty laundry won't be aired for all to see, and seek God's restorative power in our lives?

PRAYER

Close the session with prayer.

Father, You have the power to restore and rebuild what has been damaged or destroyed in our lives. We look to You to make this power known both in and through us in all areas where we need Your help. Give us boldness and courage to fully live out our purpose and calling. In Christ's name, amen.

DAY 1
HIT THE STREETS

YOU MIGHT AS WELL BE HONEST; GOD ALREADY KNOWS

Never compare your spiritual life to someone else's. Never measure your spiritual walk by how well or how badly someone else is doing. Some guys want to say, "Well, at least I don't do what he does. I must be a better Christian than him."

The moment we start thinking like that, pride will trip us up. Sometimes we lie even when we pray. It would be much better to go before God and say, "I think I like You" or even "I'm angry with You" than to be fake before the God of the universe.

You might think you'd feel uncomfortable saying that. Would you feel more comfortable lying? Keep in mind that God won't stand for untruths.

If your world has imploded, don't go around saying, "Everything is fine," because it's not fine. If you've collapsed, you're not OK. If your life has caved in, you need more than the standard three-minute prayer: "Lord, thank You for this. Thank You for that. Bless me with this. Help me do that. In Jesus's name, amen."

God says, "I'm tired of that. That's not really the truth. Your life is falling apart. You've got a pornographic mind. You're not loving others. You love what I do for you more than you love Me for who I am. That's what I want to talk about. I want to talk about those hurts and those sins. I want to get down to the heart of the matter. Do you really love Me?"

Some guys are living an inauthentic, fake Christianity, while others are living a proud Christianity that says, "I'm better than those other guys." When you come clean with God, He can come clean with you. Here are three ways to be honest with God.

1. BE TRUTHFUL

You might as well be honest. God knows the truth. When you pray, reveal the truth. It will help you and God get on the same page faster.

2. BE AUTHENTIC

Superheroes exist in movies, not in everyday life. We all have struggles, doubts, and fears. We've all failed. An authentic relationship with God and with yourself will open you up to the help you need and God wants to give it to you. Don't aim for superhero; aim for spiritual greatness. Only God can get you there.

3. DO WHAT YOU CAN

It's OK if you need to tell Jesus in prayer, "Lord, I don't know what to say." Remember that He knows your needs before you express them (see Matt. 6:8). Too many times we aim too high, saying, "I'm going to pray for thirty straight minutes." Then, when we get two minutes in and don't know what to say, we quit. Admit where you are. Start there and do what you can. Don't settle, but don't bite off more than you can chew either. Talk to Jesus like you talk to a friend. Pause to listen. Don't be afraid of silence. Pray with your Bible open. Turn off your phone. Ask Him to speak to you. Ultimately, just do what you can do and God will help you grow over time. But you won't grow if you don't try or if you quit.

LACE 'EM UP

Let's get honest with God this week! On another piece of paper or in a journal make two columns. On the left column write "Blessings." Then list every blessing in your life you can think of (it might even take multiple pages). On the right column write "Confessions." Then confess the places in your life where you've fallen short. Writing out our blessings helps us see just how much God has already done. Writing out our confessions helps us get right with God. He already knows all of these things, but He just loves talking with you!

DAY 2
DOUBLE OR NOTHING

Many of us have been challenged by powerful sermons we've heard or camps we've attended, and we've responded in a genuine way. We have good spiritual intentions, make well-meaning spiritual promises, and pray great spiritual vows, only to find we don't carry them out. Our lives may even implode when we try.

When our lives implode, many of us stop and sift through the rubble. Instead of looking to Christ and the redemption and forgiveness He offers, at worst, we turn back to our old ways of life and thinking. At best, we just sit paralyzed in our poor decisions and miss the fullness of life Jesus has for us.

Read the following words of Jesus and answer the questions.

I am the vine, you are the branches;
he who abides in Me and I in him, he bears
much fruit, for apart from Me you can do nothing.
JOHN 15:5

What do you think Jesus meant when He said to abide in Him? (Look up the word "abide" if you don't know what it means.)

What happens when we make abiding in Christ an ongoing part of our lives?

Abide means "to hang out with." That's it. When a branch abides in the vine, it remains connected to the vine. As soon as it's cut off, the branch stops producing fruit. Why? Because the source of its life was the vine. To hang out with or remain connected to Jesus Christ is the secret to your eternal significance and productivity.

Read Luke 22:31-34. Peter claimed he would remain with Jesus. However, he denied Jesus soon after. What led Peter to deny Jesus?

When are you tempted to deny you're with Jesus?

Peter had every intention of staying true to Jesus when he told Him he would never deny Him. However, Peter lacked the humility he needed to truly abide in Christ. Pride separates us from an abiding relationship with Jesus because pride says we can do things on our own. Pride says we're stronger than we actually are. Pride takes over our lives and dominates our thoughts. Humility is the foundation for an abiding connection to Jesus. Humility admits, "I can do nothing without Jesus."

In what ways does humility motivate us to abide in Christ?

Many men, young, old, and everywhere in between, understand and share Peter's attitude. We trust in our abilities, personalities, power, intelligence, and strength. But like Peter, we have to learn that lasting impact comes only through Christ in us. Some of us fail in big ways, as Peter did. Others fail in small ways. But we all have to learn the same lesson, no matter what the Teacher has to do to get it across. That lesson is the necessity of depending on and abiding in Jesus Christ's position, ability, authority, power, wisdom, and strength instead of our own.

Once you learn that lesson, you'll no longer make excuses for what you can't do. Rather, like Peter when he later preached to thousands, you'll discover that God can use you in remarkable ways, even beyond what you hoped or thought possible.

If Peter had sought to intentionally abide with Jesus and trust in Him, how could His moment of failure have been different?

Read John 21:15-17. How did Jesus respond to Peter's failings? What does Jesus tell us when we fail?

Notice that when Jesus restored Peter, He didn't rehash Peter's sin and failings. He didn't sift through the rubble with Peter. If we're truly repentant, our sin is as far away from us as the east is from the west (see Ps. 103:12). Once Peter reconnected to Jesus and began abiding in Him, he understood that he was forgiven.

It's the same with us. God takes the mess we made and starts building a new foundation on top of it. He cleans up the rubble and forgets it was ever there. When we stop and linger to look at the old broken pieces, we're taking a man-centered perspective of our sin. Jesus wants more for us. Abiding in Jesus fills us with joy. We'll never live in the joy He's given us if we're stuck staring at the rubble.

What changed about Peter's life when he understood that Jesus loved him and had completely forgiven him?

Read Acts 2:1-39. What needs to change in your heart or mind in order for you to express boldness like Peter did in these verses?

The same Peter on the beach was the same Peter at Pentecost. Yes, the same Peter who so often put his foot in his mouth. The same Peter who kept messing up, making promises he couldn't keep, afraid of what the Jews would say, scared of going public with his faith, and actually denied the Lord. Peter not only stood up, but he also spoke up. His sermon on the day of Pentecost brought three thousand people to faith in Christ. And listen to his very public confession:

Let all the house of Israel know for certain that God has made
Him both Lord and Christ—this Jesus whom you crucified.
ACTS 2:36

Peter publicly reversed his failure. That's what I call a turnaround!

Read the following verse.

Instead of your shame you will have a double portion,
And instead of humiliation they will
shout for joy over their portion.
Therefore they will possess a double portion in their land,
Everlasting joy will be theirs.
ISAIAH 61:7

What joy can we find when we stop sifting through the rubble? In what areas of your life do you need to stop looking through broken pieces?

The phrase "double or nothing" means a debt will either be canceled if a person wins a bet or doubled if they lose. God doesn't call you to gamble, but He asks you to live by faith in His promises. He offers you a double-or-nothing opportunity. If you choose to repent of the sins you've committed and serve Him in an honest, humble, abiding way, He will give you double. Or you can stick to your own strength and continue to get nothing. It's your choice. It's not a gamble. It's an offer based in an abiding love that lasts forever.

PRAY

Pray about anything in your life that may have been harmed by your failures, causing you to experience loss or lack. Ask God to give you a right heart aligned under Him. Not a perfect heart, but as Jesus illustrated with Peter, an honest, authentic heart. Then ask Him to restore to you double or even more of what you've lost in the past.

DAY 3
COCK-A-DOODLE-DO

Jesus told Peter the rooster would crow after he denied Jesus three times. After Peter heard the cock-a-doodle-do and realized he had betrayed the Lord, he went away and hid, ashamed of what he had done.

Peter may have thought the rooster's crow signaled the final curtain on his ability to serve the Lord. But when do roosters crow? Roosters crow to indicate a brand-new day. Peter was about to get a brand-new opportunity, despite the fact that he had a colossal failure and a prideful spirit.

Read Jesus's words to Peter (also known as Simon):

"Simon, Simon, look out. Satan has asked to sift you like wheat. But I have prayed for you that your faith may not fail. And you, when you have turned back, strengthen your brothers."
LUKE 22:31-32 (CSB)

Jesus prayed for Peter. Were the prayers of Jesus answered? Give support for your answer.

Jesus prayed for Peter. Scripture tells us He also prays for us (see John 17:20-23). Do you know what would happen to us if Jesus weren't praying for us? Peter went very low, but he would have gone a lot lower if Jesus hadn't prayed for him. The same is true for us. None of us know how low we would go if Jesus's prayers didn't keep us from going there.

No matter what your low point has been, you probably haven't done what Peter did, publicly denying any association with Jesus. Three times! That's about as low as anyone can go.

If there's hope for Peter, then there's hope for everyone. If Jesus wouldn't let Peter use his failure as an excuse to walk away and forget it, he won't let us walk away from His purposes for our lives. God has something better for us than reliving the worst moments of our lives over and over again.

Jesus prayed that Peter's faith wouldn't fail, and it didn't. Peter was able to be restored.

Jesus said after Peter's restoration that he would strengthen his brothers (Luke 22:32). What could God do with our failures if, instead of focusing on them, we used them to benefit others?

What are some ways we can strengthen each other as brothers?

Are you actively seeking ways to strengthen the guys around you? If so, what are you doing? If not, what can you start doing?

Peter couldn't begin to strengthen his brothers until he first came clean with Jesus. Over the charcoal fire Peter had to admit to Jesus that he had failed. Peter wasn't a hero. He wasn't a superstar. When Peter humbly admitted to Jesus that he was a weak and fallible man, Jesus forgave him and recommissioned him.

Peter first had to come clean with Jesus. He had to be authentic. Then Jesus said, "I have a place for you. Feed My lambs." That's called grace.

Peter was honest and told Jesus what Jesus already knew. Even if your world is broken, if you'll be authentic with God, He can use you, bless you, and guide you to do all the things you've wanted Him to do in and through you. He's faithful to forgive those who ask.

How does this account of Jesus's conversation with Peter give you courage to be honest with Him?

Read 1 John 1:9. Why is confession more valuable than dwelling on failures of the past?

Restoration is available to us. All we have to do is ask. We don't have to live with the guilt and shame of a broken foundation. Jesus will begin rebuilding the moment we ask. If we confess, He's faithful to forgive and cleanse us from all unrighteousness. That's restoration.

Have you failed Jesus lately? Don't let the failure keep you from running to Him. For all his failures, when Peter saw the resurrected Jesus from the boat, he jumped in the water and swam to greet Him (see John 21:7). No matter what you've done. You don't have to stay there. You can run to Jesus and accept His restoration and forgiveness.

Read 1 John 4:18. Who has the ability to give perfect love? What does God's perfect love do in our lives?

Only God loves perfectly. If you'll receive His love, He will remove the fear of failure, regrets, and inabilities, replacing them with His acceptance, grace, and mercy. This reality frees you to love and serve, abiding in Him as He develops more of His character in you each day. As that happens, He takes all of our experiences—the good, the bad, and the ugly—and turns them into a platform for service to Him. He takes us and uses us to build His church and further His kingdom, just as He used Peter.

What would you pursue for God if you knew you couldn't fail?

Fear holds us back from living in full faith. How does the gospel of Christ—the truest expression of perfect love—remove fear and replace it with courage?

If God loved you so much that He gave His only Son so that you could go to heaven (see John 3:16), He loves you enough to forgive any failure or sin in your life. His love provides strength and courage to live boldly and to risk all for the advancement of His kingdom and glory on earth.

What is something that only God can do to take your failure of yesterday and turn it around for His glory today?

PRAY

Ask God to give you a full realization of His perfect gift of love for you. Come clean with God about your spiritual walk. He already knows. Receive His forgiveness and grace. Allow Him to build you up in His love and mercy, committed to looking ahead and no longer lingering in the past.

NO MORE EXCUSES

BE THE MAN GOD MADE YOU TO BE!

TONY EVANS

SESSION 7

NO MORE HALF STEPPING

START

Welcome to Session 7 of *No More Excuses*.

Last week as you saw the dangers of sifting through the rubble, you also saw that God can build a new foundation on top of sin and brokenness.

As you read about sifting through the rubble, what stories of redemption came to mind?

All in. God wants your entire commitment, dedication, focus, and effort. Ever heard of a healthy professional athlete who shows up for only half of the practices all season long? Me either. That athlete would either be released or fans and the local media would probably constantly remind him that giving his full effort is part of the deal. Giving our full effort to the advancement of God's kingdom agenda is part of our deal too. Far too many of us offer God a half-stepping approach to spiritual development and then expect God to show up and secure the victories we need. It doesn't work that way.

What would happen if you only showed up to half of your classes?

How do you feel when you're in a group project at school and someone in your group only gives a half-hearted effort to the assignment?

If you want to make a great impact and have spiritual significance, you need to go all in. Effort. Consistency. Dedication. Hard work. Diligence. These are the markers of a kingdom man, young, old, and everywhere in between, who lives with no more excuses. Let's learn together what it means to go all in for God.

Ask someone to pray before watching the video teaching.

WATCH

NOTE: So many young men are all in, wherever they are. When they are at church they are all in. But when they get around other influences, they are all in there. Use this session to help them see that to be all in with God, they have to choose to not be all in elsewhere.

Fill in the blanks to follow along as you watch video Session 7.

The missing key to seeing God move in the life of a man is _____.

> I urge you, brethren, by the mercies of God, to present your bodies a living and holy sacrifice, acceptable to God, which is your spiritual service of worship.
> ROMANS 12:1

We will forever be giving _____ when we do not allow ourselves to be owned by the Master.

Holy: to be set apart as unique or special.

> Do not be conformed to this world, but be transformed by the renewing of your mind, so that you may prove what the will of God is, that which is good and acceptable and perfect.
> ROMANS 12:2

You can't think like the _____ thinks if you want to get what _____ has to offer.

Every day you get up, you've got to let _____ know He owns you.

We allow our _____ to be submitted to His direction. We allow Him to _____ our _____.

MAN UP

Use the following questions to discuss the video teaching.

Read the following verse together.

Therefore, brothers, by the mercies of God, I urge you
to present your bodies as a living sacrifice, holy and
pleasing to God; this is your spiritual worship.
ROMANS 12:1 (HCSB)

When the Titanic struck the iceberg, the man on lookout was missing one important tool—the binoculars. Without the binoculars the lookout crewman wasn't able to detect the iceberg and warn the captain of the upcoming danger in time. As a result, when the ship struck ice, a hole was ripped open in its side, allowing water to enter and sink the massive vessel. One missing tool created a catastrophe. Similarly, when we seek to live our life apart from the wisdom and security of full surrender to God, catastrophes ensue. Surrender allows each of us to live our lives in alignment with God's will.

Dr. Evans defined *surrender* as "placing all of our strength at God's disposal." How would you explain to a friend the concept of surrender in everyday terms?

During Old Testament times the priests made regular animal sacrifices as acts of worship on behalf of the people. These sacrifices included the killing of an animal on an altar. In no situations did the animal die on the altar, only to get back up, hobble down, and head back out to pasture. When something is dead, it's dead.

Yet that's exactly what most of us do with our spiritual sacrifice of surrender to God. We crawl onto the altar and tell God we're fully His, only to return later to our own thoughts, ways, and desires. We crawl back down off the altar when we want to, only to hop back on it when it's convenient, when we attend church, or when we have a crisis and we need God's intervention.

Why do we so often give half-hearted effort in our sacrifice to God?

When Paul instructed us to present our bodies as a living and holy sacrifice, what percentage of our time, talents, and treasure was he talking about? Explain your answer.

Fully surrendering to God causes Him to invade our lives in ways we might not be comfortable with initially. However, as He moves and works in us, He transforms us into the guy He wants us to be. As we surrender, God will show up and work in and through us to influence others for His kingdom purposes. Not only that, but we'll experience what it's like to be used for His plans on earth. Only by surrendering can we discover His plan for our lives.

When has God shown you that His ways are far superior to your own?

Dr. Evans used the example of dishes that are set apart for special use. Unlike everyday dishes, these dishes sit in a cabinet or remain on display, to be used for a holiday or special guests only. This example illustrates what it means to be holy and set apart by God for His special, unique purposes.

What are some ways we disqualify ourselves from special use by God?

Many shortcomings disqualify us from God's use. First and foremost is a lack of surrender to His will and purposes for our lives. There's no such thing as half surrender. God has a great plan for you, but you hold the key to whether He will carry out that plan in your life. That key is called surrender.

What's one small step you can take this week to increase your level of surrender to God?

PRAYER
Close the session with prayer.

Father, in a world full selfishness, You ask us to surrender. You ask us to lay down our ambitions, dreams, and desires and to replace them with Yours. We want to do that, but at times it's hard. Will You guide us in the process of learning how to surrender more fully to You in every area of our lives? In Christ's name, amen.

DAY I
HIT THE STREETS

THE BLESSINGS OF BEING ALL IN

Read Matthew 5:3-12.

These verses are called the Beatitudes. In this teaching are eight distinct things that Jesus called blessed. These eight blessings are markers of people who live authentic, committed lives of faithfulness and obedience to Him. They can be summarized into three clear groupings; attitudes toward ourselves, God, and others. Let's look at all three.

I. A PROPER ATTITUDE TOWARD SELF

Kingdom men, young , old, and everywhere in between, who are blessed by God maintain a proper attitude toward themselves. They're "poor in spirit" (v. 3). They recognize their complete dependence on God. To be poor in spirit is the opposite of being rich in pride. The happiness that comes to those who see their spiritual poverty is that "theirs is the kingdom of heaven" (v. 3). They're the ones who have their prayers answered, who see God intervene in life's circumstances, and who enjoy their Christian walk.

These guys not only see themselves as poor in spirit but also mourn over their sinfulness (see v. 4). When Peter was confronted with his sin, he broke down and wept (see Mark 14:72). When Paul recognized his sin, he cried out in spiritual pain (see Rom. 7:14-24). When we feel the pain of conviction over our sin and repent, then we experience God's comfort.

2. A PROPER ATTITUDE TOWARD GOD

This type of man is also meek, or gentle (see Matt. 5:5), and they "hunger and thirst for righteousness" (v. 6). Meekness doesn't mean the same thing as weakness. The term referred to bringing wild horses under control. The picture is of a trainer taking an uncontrollable, rebellious horse and bringing it into submission. When the process is finished, the horse is said to be meek. The horse doesn't lose its strength, but its strength is under the control of the trainer. The blessing for being meek or gentle is found in verse 5: "they shall inherit the earth." Only meek Christians will see the richest blessings God has to offer them in their lives.

3. A PROPER ATTITUDE TOWARD OTHERS

Kingdom men who are blessed by God possess a proper attitude toward others. They are merciful (see v. 7) and put grace into action. Just as God looked down and had compassion on us in our hopeless, sinful condition, we must also show compassion to others. The blessing for those who show mercy is that they'll also be receivers of mercy. God will not give us what we are unwilling to give to others.

The man God blesses is also "pure in heart" (v. 8). He don't have to edit his life. With a guy like this, what you see is what you get. The blessing for the pure in heart is that "they shall see God" (v. 8). That is, they'll see God operating in their lives.

Kingdom men are also peacemakers (see v. 9). They pursue unity, not division. They seek to pull people together, not tear them apart. God will ensure a strong, vital testimony for a guy who keeps "the unity of the Spirit in the bond of peace" (Eph. 4:3).

Finally, kingdom men are "persecuted for the sake of righteousness" (Matt. 5:10). The idea here is to look so much like Christ in our actions and attitudes that what happened to Christ happens to us and for the same reason it happened to Him. The blessing for men who are persecuted and insulted for identifying with Jesus is a great reward in heaven and blessing on earth.

LACE 'EM UP

Let's go all in this week! Another way to look at these three categories is the old acrostic JOY—Jesus, Others, Yourself. Take some pages in your journal or on a sheet of paper and write these three words—Jesus, Others, Yourself—at the top of the page. Ask yourself this question, "Where do I have the wrong attitude?" Spend some time in prayer, then write the responses the Lord brings to your mind and heart on the pages. You can do this exercise all at once or over the course of three days. When you are finished with your lists, pray over them again and ask God to help you go all in and have the right heart and attitude toward Jesus, others, and yourself.

DAY 2
THE CHICKEN AND THE PIG

A chicken and a pig were walking down the street one day and came to a grocery store. A sign in the window said, "Bacon and eggs needed." The chicken looked at the pig and said, "Let's help out!"

The pig responded, "You must be crazy. For you that's just a contribution, but for me that's a total commitment!"

That's the way a lot of guys feel about kingdom life: "Hey, I don't mind contributing a little here and there. But let's not go overboard. Let's not go as far as total commitment." Total commitment to God and His kingdom sounds a little too risky for a lot of guys, as if the kingdom life will cost them too much. So they give a part of themselves to Christ but hold back the rest in case kingdom life gets too demanding.

Read the following verses and answer the questions.

> And one of them, an expert in the law, asked a question to test him: "Teacher, which command in the law is the greatest?" He said to him, "Love the Lord your God with all your heart, with all your soul, and with all your mind. This is the greatest and most important command. The second is like it: Love your neighbor as yourself."
> MATTHEW 22:35-39 (CSB)

What are some reasons we stop short of loving God with all our heart, soul, and mind?

List practical ways we can love God with all our heart, soul, and mind.

Which of these two commands do you find hardest to obey, loving God or loving other people? Explain your answer.

Paul called us to offer ourselves as living sacrifices to God:

> Therefore, brothers, by the mercies of God, I urge you
> to present your bodies as a living sacrifice, holy and
> pleasing to God; this is your spiritual worship.
> ROMANS 12:1 (HCSB)

Paul was commanding whole-life devotion to God. By definition a sacrifice was killed, yet Paul called us to remain living sacrifices. We're literally to be the walking dead. How is this possible? Paul's description of his own life offers insight:

> I have been crucified with Christ; and it is
> no longer I who live, but Christ lives in me.
> GALATIANS 2:20

Crucification was a painful and shameful way to die. It was the Roman way of making sure someone was fully dead. When Paul said he was "crucified with Christ," he meant his desires, goals, and preferences were dead and had been replaced with God's will for him. God's goals had become Paul's goals. God's desires had become Paul's desires. The only life Paul had was the life of Christ. That's why no one could intimidate this man (see Phil. 1:21-24).

Think about your desires, goals, and preferences. Are any of them out of sync with God's desires, goals, and preferences for you? If so, what are they?

What would it look like to crucify your will in these areas to pursue Christ wholeheartedly?

Which of these desires, goals, and preferences would you be most tempted to hold on to even though you know it's outside God's plan?

Notice that Paul never wrote in Scripture, "If you want to be committed, go to church." Worship starts with the commitment of our lives, not with our church attendance or being part of a small group. Although we should go to church and participate in Bible studies, they, in and of themselves, don't fulfill our commitment of total sacrifice to the Lord. It's tragic that so many people worship God on Sunday or participate in small groups but ignore Him—or even worse, worship themselves—the rest of the week. When we're living sacrifices, every activity of our lives becomes an act of worship. To worship means to give glory. It's what we think about, what we invest our time in, what we focus our lives on, and what we actually do with our lives. Worship encompasses everything and it isn't just limited to Sundays.

When we refuse to give God all of ourselves, whom are we really worshiping? How does that reality change the way you think about pursuing your own desires?

What are some ways we worship ourselves in our world today?

How can we counter this trend to surrender to God's call to full life devotion?

The greatest men in the kingdom of God understand that life isn't all about them. We're on a team, and our owner is the Lord. We play for Him. We produce for Him. We create for Him. We invest effort for Him. After all, He owns us. He paid the price. He covers, protects, and provides. What better way to honor God than by giving Him everything we have?

The problem is that many of us have settled for half-hearted worship of God, which is actually fully devoted worship of ourselves. When we make ourselves the center of our lives, we miss out on the life God has for us. We make excuses and refuse to give God what He requires—all we are. In doing this, we settle for half a life. God has promised us a full, abundant life (see John 10:10), but to take hold of that life, we must surrender to Him.

How could a group of guys like this Bible study group help you remain fully devoted to God?

Do any other guys know the ways you struggle with half stepping? Do they have permission to speak into your life with honestly and clarity?

Commitment is contagious. When one athlete works harder in the gym or plays better on the field, the other players often improve their performance as well. We need others to help us walk the Christian life. Many of us suffer because we force ourselves to be on an island. God has given us community to pursue Him together. Take advantage of it.

What's one way you'll display deeper commitment to God this week?

PRAY

Ask God to show you any areas of your life in which you're holding back from a full commitment to Him. Ask Him to give you the desire to surrender your heart, soul, and mind to Him and to do whatever it takes to lead you to that commitment.

DAY 3
FOLLOW-THROUGH

Follow-through is critical in many sports, such as baseball, tennis, and golf, as well as for the quarterback in football. Follow-through means continuing the motion all the way through to the end, even after the ball has left the hand, racket, or club. If you follow through in baseball, the bat stays in contact with the ball for the longest possible period of time, thereby propelling the ball with greater force and accuracy. Home runs result from excellent follow-through, not from half swings.

If we are going to stop half stepping and live with greater commitment to Christ, we need to understand the importance of follow through. We need to grasp the importance of going to the full extent in our faith by expressing it in our actions.

Hebrews 11:6 says, "Without faith it is impossible to please [God]." To believe in what you can see requires no faith; it's right there in front of you. But to be convinced that what you can't see is real and to have as much confidence in its reality as you do in what you can see, hear, taste, touch, and smell is genuine faith. In other words, authentic faith is required for you to follow through with confidence on your commitment to God.

Read the following verses.

> Faith, if it has no works, is dead, being by itself.
> But someone may well say, "You have faith and
> I have works; show me your faith without the
> works, and I will show you my faith by my works."
> JAMES 2:17-18

Why must faith be accompanied by action to be genuine faith?

Sometimes very bold, or crazy, baseball players walk up to the plate and point their bat over the outfield wall, predicting what's to come. The player is trying to intimidate the pitcher by declaring that he's about to hit a home run. He may be seeking to convince himself of it as well. Athletes routinely visualize success prior to taking the field, hill, court or track.

Like sports, faith requires follow through. Visualization, or imagining what will happen, isn't a bad thing. God uses our desires to call us into action. However, if all we ever do is imagine all the things we're going to do for God but never actually do them, we're half stepping our way through our faith journey. God isn't interested in our half-hearted intentions. Faith requires action; anything less is disobedience. This principle isn't limited to our lives at church. It extends to our homes and schools as well.

Take an inventory of your faith-based actions. On a scale from 1 to 10, what level of follow-through are you living out in regard to your faith?

0   1   2   3   4   5   6   7   8   9   10
No follow through   Complete follow through

When you struggle to follow through in your faith, what is it that keeps you from following through?

Is there a faith action you're visualizing right now? What would be required to put it into practice? What steps could you take this week?

Can you identify an area in which you aren't following through in your life right now? What's one step you could take to correct your half stepping?

Consider your school, extracurricular activities, even your responsibilities around your house. What elements of your life require you to follow through?

The point of these question isn't to make you feel guilty but to call you to action. Consider them a nudge to get into the game. When guys take what God is placing on their hearts and move that urge to action, the kingdom benefits. When we give full-hearted effort in all that we're involved in and connected to, we recognize that we're not really doing it for other people but for God (see Eph. 6:7).

The faith we're to exercise as Christians has to be more than talk. James illustrated the point this way:

> If a brother or sister is without clothing and in need
> of daily food, and one of you says to them, "Go in peace,
> be warmed and be filled," and yet you do not give them
> what is necessary for their body, what use is that?
> JAMES 2:15-16

The benefits of faith don't happen just because we say the right things but because we execute the right actions based on what we believe and say. If you're feeling defeated today or if you aren't fully living out your greatness and destiny, maybe you're suffering from the problem many of James's readers suffered from: belief without practice. As James argued, that kind of faith is useless to God.

Describe a time when, in faith, you acted with complete follow-through on something. What were the results?

Based on today's study, record one step you plan to take to have follow-through in what you do.

Follow-through ushers you into the type of kingdom impact God has called you to make. Imagine that you owned a professional baseball team and scouted a player who you knew could hit the ball. You chose to offer this player a large contract, but after you sign him, he choses not to hit the ball. Would you be pleased? What if he chose never to swing again? That player would soon be off the team.

God doesn't kick us off His eternal team; salvation comes with eternal security. However, He limits His use of us in His kingdom program when we refuse to walk by faith with complete follow-through in our actions. No one would question a coach who benched a player who never swung at a ball. Similarly, we shouldn't question God when He chooses to use others who demonstrate greater faith through their actions.

PRAY

Read Psalm 90:17 and ask God to clarify the kingdom work He wants you to do. Invite Him to increase your faith as you take steps to obey Him. You may want to record the steps you take along with the ways you see God respond to your actions. Use your testimony to spur yourself to action on days when you doubt and to inspire others to move in obedience to God's call.

SESSION 8

NO MORE STANDING ON THE SIDELINES

START

Welcome to Session 8 of *No More Excuses*.

As we head into this final week, let's think about how far we've come.

You've made it to the final week. What has been the most impactful lesson you've learned from this study?

In 2017, Philadelphia Eagles were riding high at 11-2 when their season seemingly came to a screeching halt. Their starting quarterback, Carson Wentz, tore his ACL and would be out for the remainder of the year. Nobody saw coming what happened next. Backup QB Nick Foles, who had been a journeyman in the NFL up to that point, replaced Wentz and guided the Eagles to the Super Bowl against the dreaded New England Patriots. Not many pundits gave them much of a chance, but Foles lead the Eagles to a 41-33 victory and was named the game's MVP. Now, imagine after Wentz went down, the coach calling Foles to get in the game and him replying, "Nah, coach. I'm good on the bench!" This sounds, ridiculous, right? But many of us do this everyday. God is calling us to get in the game, but we're content to just stay on the sidelines.

What's one reason we become content on the sidelines of life?

The Eagles would not have won the Super Bowl if not for Foles's willingness to get in the game and play his best. Men, young, old and everywhere in between, God has a plan for you. You don't belong on the sidelines. You belong in the game. This week we're going to look at how you can take part in everything God intends for you to do by fully engaging on the field of your life.

Ask someone to pray before watching the video teaching.

WATCH

NOTE: This is your last week. Thank the guys for participating in this study. Challenge them to step up and start living out 1 Corinthians 13:11. They don't have to leave adolescence behind entirely, but encourage them to begin to put away childish things and embrace their future as a man.

Use these statements to follow along as you watch video Session 8.

No more _____. No more living an _____ life.

Nehemiah became a man of _____, influence, perseverance, _____, unwilling to compromise.

You are the one to see the _____ of the culture.

Nehemiah didn't make the distinction between _____ and _____. He was going to bring the spiritual into the secular.

There's a _____ in the spiritual realm that's causing _____ in the physical realm.

You've been called to be a man of _____, not just be a man by nomenclature.

I'm going to _____ _____ for the divine principles of God, and I'm not going to give any more _____.

MAN UP

Use the following questions to discuss the video teaching.

Read the following verse together.

> For this purpose also I labor, striving according
> to His power, which mightily works within me.
> COLOSSIANS 1:29

Strive means to "diligently pursue an outcome." It involves hard work. Persistence. Effort. Consistency. And a whole lot of just plain determination. In this passage Paul explained that his striving was done in the power of Christ, which strongly worked in him. Through His strength Paul was able to accomplish more than he ever would have on his own.

When have you had to admit that you didn't have the strength necessary to complete a task? Who came to your aid?

In the video Dr. Evans summarized the plotline of the movie *The Matrix,* in which a computer programmer is called on to literally save the world. He has a choice to make. If he takes the red pill offered to him, he will leave behind everything he knows as real and enter a new reality. But he will be positioned to carry out his destiny as "The One."

Neo, the computer programmer, knows what will happen if he takes the pill. He also knows that the man offering him the pill believes in him enough to offer it. The combined force of this knowledge gives him the courage to get off the sidelines and into the battle. We too have a red pill—the blood of Christ that works powerfully in us and gives us the ability to accomplish what can be done only through Him.

What has Christ empowered you to do that you never could have done on your own?

How do we honor Jesus and the sacrifice He made on our behalf when we take hold of the power He gives us, get off the sidelines, and enter the game?

In what areas of your life is God calling you to get into the game?

Dr. Evans used the example of a bowler who has the right look and equipment, but can't knock down the pins, to represent a believer who looks good on the outside but lacks true spiritual power. Looking good doesn't automatically equate with leaving a legacy of positive impact. We have all the necessary equipment. Jesus has given us all we need to make a game-changing impact. To do that, we have to leave the sidelines behind and play the game in His power.

Why do we settle for looking the part of a believer? How could the working of Christ's kingdom power in us make an impact in your daily life?

We must understand that making a kingdom impact involves more than looking the part. God is seeking guys who truly influence the people around them for the kingdom of God. He's looking for one, like Nehemiah, who risks his life to build God's kingdom in the world. Nehemiah was a government worker, not someone we think of as being a spiritual giant. Yet when Nehemiah saw a God-sized problem, he took a risk and asked to be put in the game. God is looking for bold obedience. He's looking for someone, like you, who will follow Him wherever He leads you.

Legacies are built of small acts of greatness stacked on top of one another. What's one small act of greatness you can do this week for the kingdom of God?

PRAYER

Close the session with prayer.

Father, we want to make an impact. We want to be a part of Your team to lead this world to You. Help us get off the sidelines and start working toward the goals You've established for us to live out.

DAY 1
HIT THE STREETS
THREE KEYS TO
POSITIVE IMPACT

Nehemiah had a tremendous impact on his entire nation at a critical time in their history. His life modeled what it meant to live for the kingdom of God. We can increase our positive impact for the kingdom of God when we seek to apply the following three spiritual qualities from Nehemiah's life.

1. A MAN OF FAITH

To be a man of faith, you must have a bigger view of God than you do of the enemy (see Eph. 6:12). If you have a bigger view of the enemy, he will dominate you. Wind can't move an iceberg because most of an iceberg is beneath the surface of the water. But the current can move an iceberg, even in the face of a fierce wind, because the pull of the current is stronger than the push of the wind. If the pull of God is stronger in our lives than the push of the enemy, God's influence will win out.

Dr. Evans has been intimidated at various times, especially when his life was being threatened. But if he ever allowed the threats of the enemy to control him, he would have quit his ministry a long time ago. If we're going to do anything of lasting value for the kingdom, we must be people of faith. There will be times in your life when you'll need to stand shoulder to shoulder with other guys who believe and take a stand against the enemy. You'll never be counted in that number without faith.

2. A MAN OF JUSTICE

Nehemiah held the leaders of Jerusalem accountable. He didn't let God's people get away with unjust business practices, with holding their brothers in slavery, and with the wealthy oppressing the poor.

Let's be honest with one another. Some of the things we as Christians tolerate aren't even on the borderline. They're just wrong. If we're going to make a godly impact, we must be people of justice like Nehemiah. We must practice justice, insist on it, and fight for it when necessary. The question we need to ask ourselves is, *What does God think?* not, *What will people think?*

3. A MAN OF PERSEVERANCE

If you want to make an impact, don't stop doing what God wants you to do. Don't give up the dream God gave you just because trouble shows up. Keep rebuilding. Don't let other people knock you off the wall. Too many of us hear the world say, "You can't make any difference. Don't even try. It's not worth the effort." Who says? I'll tell you who says. No one with any real authority. The problem is that we're listening to those voices rather than the voice of God.

Keep on going. Don't let people who have no spiritual perspective stop you. When you persevere in what God has called you to do, you have the opportunity to make an eternal impact for His kingdom.

LACE 'EM UP

Let's have a positive impact this week! More than likely, at some point, you'll be tempted to quit this week. Maybe it's on that last lap on the track and you see that the coach isn't looking, so you stop to walk. Or maybe, you notice just before you turn off the lawn mower that you missed a spot. In those instances don't quit, keep going.

More importantly than that, you may have a friend you feel will never see the light of God's grace in his life. Don't give up on him either. This week be diligent to pray for that friend. Pray that God gives you an opportunity to show him love, kindness, and grace. Remember: it's not your responsibility to save anyone. God does the saving. You just need to be faithful before others and be faithful to give a verbal witness when God opens a door to share about His love.

DAY 2
GOD'S WAYS

Nehemiah was a Jew living in Persia as a servant of Artaxerxes, the king of Persia. He was a descendant of the Israelites who had been carried into captivity by the Babylonians nearly 150 years earlier. Nehemiah had never been to Jerusalem, but his heart was there because that's where God's people and God's heart were.

Nehemiah received a distressing report from his brother about conditions in Jerusalem:

> The remnant there in the province who survived the captivity
> are in great distress and reproach, and the wall of Jerusalem
> is broken down and its gates are burned with fire.
> NEHEMIAH 1:3

Nehemiah was crushed, not only for the sake of his people but also for the sake of his God, because he knew these conditions were an offense to God's name.

Nehemiah didn't start pushing for a political solution. Nehemiah didn't try to get the right person in office, get the right laws passed, or get the right programs in place. Nehemiah knew better, so he immediately bowed before God with tears, prayer, and fasting (see v. 4). He also turned to God's Word for the right perspective on his problem.

If you want to make an impact, you don't start with political, social, or economic solutions, although all three of these later came into play in Nehemiah's situation. No, you need to fall before God in fasting and prayer and go to the Word.

Read the following verses and record the common element in all of them.

Ezra 8:21

Esther 4:16

Daniel 9:3

Jonah 3:5

Matthew 4:1-2

Matthew 17:20-21

Acts 9:8-9

Acts 13:2-3

Fasting and prayer are recurring themes throughout Scripture, particularly when an individual or a group of people were seeking to make a large impact on an entire culture or to carry out a mission of healing or service for God. When we get called into the game from the sidelines, fasting and prayer are the first plays we should run.

Does fasting always have to mean skipping meals and not eating food? From what other activities can we fast in order to focus on seeking God?

Fasting is the reduction or removal of something that brings physical gratification as you seek God for a greater spiritual need. Temporarily stopping something enjoyable, like eating, social media, or watching TV, helps us focus our attention on something better. Fasting is a means God uses to open our hearts and minds to the work He has for us.

Fasting isn't something you do casually. You can't just skip a meal or a TV show and call it a fast. Nehemiah wept as he fasted. Many biblical examples of fasting involved a repentant spirit. In letting go the power and attachment to something physical, we let God know we're serious. Our full attention, surrender, and sacrifice can then be devoted to entering God's presence and crying out to Him.

Prayer and fasting allow us to hear the Lord more clearly, but they don't just happen, you have to make time for them. Over the next few weeks, when will you take time to pray and fast? What will you fast from? What will you fast about?

Nehemiah fasted and prayed because the walls of Jerusalem had been torn down in battle. As a result, the city wasn't safe and secure. Through fasting and prayer, God led Nehemiah to action. Nehemiah mourned over the condition of the walls because he believed Jerusalem was the Lord's city that was meant to reflect His leadership and rule. To Nehemiah, the glory of the Lord was at stake.

Whatever walls are broken down in your life, your first action should be turning to God. Through prayer, fasting, and the Word, He will bring to your heart and mind the steps you must take to rebuild what has been destroyed.

Read Nehemiah 2:1-5. What did God lead Nehemiah to do about the condition of his fellow Israelites and their city?

God placed Nehemiah in the king's service. Think about where God has placed you. How could you be used for His service in those places?

Read Isaiah 58:8-9. How does God's larger perspective give Him a different vantage point for viewing our situation?

God has placed you where you are for a reason. Just as He placed Esther in the kingdom "for such a time as this" (Esther 4:14) in order to save her people from certain death, and just as He appointed Nehemiah as the cupbearer to the king (see Neh. 1:11), God has a reason He has placed you where you are. God is intentional. Never let only what you can see determine the way you feel about your significance.

We don't have the perspective to understand all God is doing in the world. We don't know what God will do with simple obedience. It's not clear to us what God will do when we share the gospel with a friend or seek to serve someone on our team. God will take those extra moments we give to the people around us and multiply them. He takes our ordinary obedience and multiplies it for kingdom impact.

Players on the sidelines don't contribute to the game. In what ways have you been passive when God is calling you to be active? How could you make an impact if you got into the game?

Is there an area of life in which you need to hear from the Lord? When will you fast and pray specifically for this need?

Who could help hold you accountable to remain in the game now that you're off the sidelines?

God knows the end from the beginning (see Isa. 46:10). He knows the plan. He knows what play to call. He's got the winning strategies for both offense and defense. And He can take you where you need to go. But being led by God requires fully seeking Him with your whole heart through fasting, prayer, and the Word. It requires demonstrating your trust in Him by following His directions for every area of your life. If you want to be a guy who makes a kingdom impact, then suit up. Get in the game. Play by His rules. His calls. And pursue His goals. His way.

PRAY

Pray about ways you can make a greater impact for the kingdom of God. Seek to be faithful where He has placed you and ask Him to show you the specific areas where He wants you to make an even greater impact for Him.

DAY 3
LEADERS LEAVE LEGACIES

If you're going to make an impact it takes spiritual leadership. I'm not talking about you wanting spiritual leadership or just talking about spiritual leadership. I don't even mean just studying the subject of spiritual leadership.

To make an impact you have to *take* spiritual leadership. You have to be proactive and not just wait around for someone else to appoint you, ask you, anoint you, or nudge you. You just do it. You lead, and by His power, you lead well.

Dr. Evans regularly challenges the men of his church to take spiritual initiative to make an impact on the world around them. He might ask you, "When was the last time you started a Bible study with your friends?" "When was the last time you prayed with someone that you knew was hurting?" "When was the last time you went to the altar at church and just got on your knees before God?" "When was the last time you talked to the person that sits next to you in class about what you learned in church the day before?"

You don't have to be a preacher to take spiritual leadership. You don't need to have graduated from college to pray with somebody. You just need to do it.

Read the following verse.

For Ezra had devoted himself to the study and observance of the Law of the LORD, and to teaching its decrees and laws in Israel.
EZRA 7:10 (NIV)

List the three actions Ezra committed to take as a leader.

1.

2.

3.

First Ezra studied what God said in His Word, as you've been doing through this Bible study. Then Ezra went a step further by applying what he had learned to his life. He practiced the principles from God's Word. He put the truths to work. Then he taught them to others. Study, practice, teach. It's as simple and straightforward as that.

Why is it important to practice what you study before you attempt to teach it to others?

Have you ever tried to teach something without having put it into practice in your life? What was the result?

Have you ever known someone who lived what they taught? What impact did that example make on you? What would it look like to imitate this person's faith (see Heb. 13:7)?

Simply put, a leader is someone who knows the way, goes the way, and shows the way. The crisis today is that too many young men are being defeated by life's problems. The reason guys are being defeated is that they don't know the Word, they don't know how to apply the Word, or they choose not to put into action what they do know.

Jesus assigned each of us the role of teaching truth when He gave the Great Commission (see Matt. 28:19-20). He called us to make disciples and teach the truth of God's Word as we go through our everyday lives. This isn't a suggestion but a calling on the lives of all Christians.

When was the most recent time you tried to explain Scripture to someone else?

Read 2 Timothy 2:1-2. Who's investing in you as a young kingdom man? Whom are you currently seeking to invest in?

Leadership is a lifestyle. It expresses itself in everything you do. It shows up in the way you handle victory and in the way you handle defeat. Leadership involves applying all of the kingdom principles and biblical teachings you've examined in this study. It takes effort. Dedication. Desire. Consistency. Service. Sacrifice. Surrender. And a whole lot more.

What are the needs of your church? Even though you are a teenager, how are you involved in meeting them?

What skills do you possess that God could put to use in your church?

Take a look at your life. Identify areas in which you're making the greatest impact and look for ways to strengthen those areas. Then identify ways you could make an even greater impact.

Greatest Impact   **More Impact Needed**

In 1989, Dr. Evans was hospitalized when the doctor thought a lump he had was cancer. The night before the surgery as he lay on that hospital bed, do you think he worried about what other people thought about him? Do you think he lay there wishing he had the newest shoes, more friends, or a larger building in which to preach? No, he didn't worry about any of that. What he wanted was the opportunity to live longer so that he could make an impact for God. He wanted to influence his children. He wanted to care for his wife in such a way that she could flourish in her career and interests. He wanted the people around him to be transformed by spiritual truths and the messages God placed on his heart each week to reach as many people as possible.

The lump wasn't cancer, and God has given him more years to serve. Yet as he enters the final season of his life, having preached for fifty years, he wants to leave a legacy of impact for the kingdom. I'm sure you do too. Leaders leave legacies. It's what we do. You've been called to God's kingdom for such a time as this—to leave an impact for His glory, blessing others, and the advancement of His agenda here on earth.

PRAY

Record a prayer to God in your own words, asking Him to develop you into the spiritual leader He wants you to be. Pray it daily.

Dear God,

_____

_____

_____

_____

_____

_____

_____

NO MORE EXCUSES

BE THE MAN GOD MADE YOU TO BE!

D-GROUP GUIDE

There is great value in going through this Bible study as an individual, but even greater value in going through it with a larger group of guys. It's possible that within the group is a smaller group of three or four guys who want to dive deeper into the content and to hold each other accountable. To this end we've provided this D-Group guide to facilitate those kinds of small groups.

WHAT IS A D-GROUP? As opposed to an open small group (meaning everyone is welcome), a D-Group is a closed group that only three or four guys join by invitation and stay in through shared commitment.

WHAT'S THE PURPOSE OF A D-GROUP? These groups are for Christian guys who desire to walk more closely with the Lord. The smaller nature of the group allows a more concentrated level of accountability and opens up discussions that are more personal than in a standard group meeting.

WHY DO I NEED A D-GROUP? We're not meant to live the Christian life alone. You'll need support as you seek to live and grow as a young kingdom man. Opening yourself up to people in a smaller environment encourages participation from you and from those who may not feel comfortable opening up in a larger group.

Additionally, D-Groups give others permission to speak into your life for encouragement, accountability, and prayer.

WHAT'S REQUIRED OF ME? The goal of these groups is deeper discipleship and accountability. Achieving this goal requires commitment. Plan to meet for one hour. Be willing to attend and participate each week. Be willing to be open and honest about your spiritual condition and about ways you're struggling. Be willing to hold what's said in the group in confidence. What's said should remain in the group as a means of building trust with one another. Finally, be willing to pray and support one another. Allow the relationships to extend beyond the group meeting itself.

HOW TO USE THESE GUIDES

A D-Group guide is provided for each week of this study. These guides are meant to be used in addition to the weekly group session. These guides work best if participants have seen the week's video teaching by Dr. Evans. Each D-Group guide is two pages and includes the following elements. There is a place to record the members of the D-Group and prayer requests on pages 156-157 of this book.

DEVOTION. Dr. Evans's sons—**Jonathan Evans,** a speaker, an author, and a chaplain for the Dallas Cowboys, and **Anthony Evans,** an author, a musician, and a worship leader—have written devotions about the weeks' topics. These short devotional thoughts are intended to lead into a time of discussion.

D-GROUP QUESTIONS. In addition to the devotion, a passage of Scripture with some commentary and three questions are provided. These open-ended questions are designed to encourage guys to open up about their struggles and successes for the purposes of growth and accountability.

SESSION I
NO MORE HIDING BEHIND THE PAST

ANTHONY EVANS

Of the four Evans kids, I'm the emotional one. I'm the guy whose feelings about the past can get so completely out of control that just thinking about my future wrecks me. In my most difficult moments, when I couldn't seem to figure out a way to move past where I'd been and the situations I'd sometimes created for myself, I would sit down with my father. He would remind me that our enemy's goal is to have us looking in the rearview mirror of our lives so much that we forget to look forward out of life's windshield.

If you're not already, within the next few years all of you will be driving. The rearview mirror is really important, especially when backing up. But behind the wheel, you spend most of your time looking through the windshield. There's nothing wrong with glancing in the rearview mirror to get perspective on what's behind. There are times when it's really helpful because the past can help us make better decisions. But if we look in the rearview mirror for too long, we fail to pay attention to what's happening now, and we set ourselves up for trouble.

That lesson has always stuck with me as a constant reminder of the perspective we should have as people seeking after God. There's a specific reason your rearview mirror is much smaller than your windshield. It's simply because what's in front of you is more important than what's behind you.

GLORY DAYS ARE AHEAD

The past can be a funny thing for guys. You may have witnessed your dad or other men sitting around talking about their glory days. Maybe that was high school, college, or when they were first married. The problem with dwelling on the glory days is that they are always seen with rose-colored glasses. Do you know what that means? It means to remember only the good stuff that happened and to cut out all that's bad or painful.

Others do just the opposite. They look back at the past and only remember the bad stuff. It could be the betrayal of a close friend, a significant loss, or a difficult obstacle. No matter how you see your past, a Christian's best days are in the future.

Consider the words of Paul, who had an eventful past:

> Brothers, I do not consider myself to have taken hold
> of it. But one thing I do: Forgetting what is behind and
> reaching forward to what is ahead, I pursue as my goal the
> prize promised by God's heavenly call in Christ Jesus.
> PHILIPPIANS 3:13-14 (HCSB)

What events in your past are you tempted to look at through rose-colored glasses? What do you look back on with hurt and frustration? How do these memories hinder progress in the present?

Why is it far more important for us to press on toward Christ? How are you doing that?

When are you most tempted to get stuck in the past? How can we help one another move forward in the present?

Close your D-Group time in prayer.

SESSION 2
NO MORE HOLDING BACK
ANTHONY EVANS

I recently became a homeowner. This is something that's many years down the road for you, but trust me, it's a big deal! My dad was there during the home-buying process to answer all of my questions. Sometimes I had to ask myself whether the painful process of trying to secure a loan to buy the house was worth it. It was more than annoying at times, but because I saw the property's value and had specific plans for what I wanted to do with the house, I decided to push through. I walked through the house verbalizing and visualizing all my plans, excited for the moment when I could start executing my vision. I wanted to start the renovations as soon as possible, but I had to complete one task before I could begin. I had to go through the process of taking ownership before beginning the process of making a change.

A lot of us want to make and see changes in our lives without taking ownership of who we are as sons of God. We hold back and wonder why we aren't able to truly lead and make changes in our lives and world. I've had the privilege of watching my father make the conscious decision not to hold back and to take full ownership of who he was created to be. This conscious decision, although hard at times, led him to make permanent renovations in his character that made him the speaker, pastor, writer, and leader you know, as well as the father and mentor I'm honored to have.

I encourage you to take ownership of who God intends for you to be without holding back, knowing that ownership leads to the ability to make permanent change.

THE GOD WHO DOESN'T HOLD BACK

He who did not spare His own Son, but delivered Him over for us all, how will He not also with Him freely give us all things?
ROMANS 8:32

God didn't withhold His Son from us, and through His Son He gives us all things. Why do we feel like we can withhold from God?

In what ways are you most likely to hold back from God, your family, your friends, and your responsibilities? What causes you to hold back in these ways?

In what ways do you need to be challenged to give more of yourself in service to God and others?

God gave what was most important to Him in order to secure our redemption. He didn't hold anything back but graciously allowed His Son to bear the shame and pain of crucifixion for us.

As we seek to follow Jesus, we hope that we become increasingly like Him, that His desires become our desires, that His thoughts become our thoughts. So we need to ask the question, "Did Jesus hold anything back?" No! Jesus gave His life in a world-changing act of grace and mercy.

Jesus took full ownership of the mission God placed before Him. He embraced it and never looked back. If we want to be like Jesus, we won't hold back. Not in our mission. Not in our schools. Not in our lives. We're all in because Jesus is all in.

Close your D-Group time in prayer.

SESSION 3
NO MORE WEAK LEADERSHIP

ANTHONY EVANS

I fly a lot for my job. At times it seems I'm in the air as much as I'm at home. I've always found it interesting that on a cloudy or rainy day when visibility is low, the pilots still know where they're going. They taxi to the end of the runway and effortlessly take off into a white mist, which from my perspective looks like a complete disaster waiting to happen. The one factor that brings relief to the anxiety I have when flying is knowing the pilots have access to an instrument panel and communication system. In that moment when nothing is clear, I trust that the pilots aren't going to lean on their own understanding.

Good pilots aren't just going to fly the plane in a direction they feel is right. They refer to the panel and communicate with the people in the control tower who can see conditions more clearly. The pilots know they're responsible for hundreds of lives, as well as the reputation of an airline, so they don't just take their seats in the cockpit and fly by what they see. Even in good weather they take their seats and then make sure they're reading the gauges correctly. More importantly, they put on their headsets and make sure they're connected to ground control. Then they begin to fly according to what they're reading and the directions provided by the people who see the bigger picture. That's the only way they can accurately measure their real distance from disaster.

God wants guys who are leaders not just because of a seat they've taken but because they take the instrument of His Word and begin to prepare for takeoff only when they're carefully and closely listening to His voice. That's the definition of a true leader.

MODEL LEADERSHIP

Remember those who led you, who spoke
the word of God to you; and considering the
result of their conduct, imitate their faith.
HEBREWS 13:7

The author of Hebrews charges us to remember those who led you and those who spoke the Word of God to you. He invites you to examine their faith and their lives and put their example into practice in your own life.

In order not to be a weak leader, we need to have strong leaders as models. Other guys your age probably look to athletes, celebrities, and social media influencers for model leadership. Though some of these people might lead lives worthy of imitation, the Bible never includes such people as examples.

The Bible calls us to follow the examples of men of faith, those who lead humble and quiet lives. The leadership we're called to follow isn't flashy and may not win the praise of society. Men worthy of imitation are those who get up early to meet with God and who love and lead their families in a sacrificial way. They're the ones who invest in the next generation, teaching young men what it means to be a man. They do their jobs with integrity and confidence. They lead in ways that the world might not notice but that the Bible commends.

In what ways do you have leadership responsibilities? How would you rate your leadership in areas where God has given it to you?

Is there an area of leadership in which God is calling you to step up? If so, what is it?

What are actions we can take to hold one another accountable for leading where we're called?

Close your D-Group time in prayer.

SESSION 4
NO MORE GOING THROUGH THE MOTIONS

ANTHONY EVANS

My father taught me the meaning of pursuing what I know I'm called to do, even when I don't feel like it. He introduced me to the concept that my feelings ultimately follow my feet. What I mean is that guys are constantly tempted to enter a place of complacency and just settle because the work required to be exceptional can seem daunting. What we forget is that it's often only after we reach the other side, after the pain of pushing through the mundane, that we truly experience the blessing of what God wants for us.

In most Bible stories there's a moment of the mundane before the miracle. Once we realize that remaining committed in the day to day ultimately leads us to the victory we desire, then and only then do our perspectives change about the challenges we're facing. As Ezekiel Elliott trains to be one the best running backs in the NFL, he runs the same drills countless times to train himself to perform well under pressure. Serena Williams serves thousands of tennis balls to an empty court in order to be the best player in the world. If either of these athletes were simply going through the motions in their training, they would perform these drills, but they wouldn't develop the heart of a champion. Their attitude wouldn't be that of a winner.

Our hearts as believers should be willing to take our mundane moments and treat them as if God is teaching us truth about our victory, even if we don't feel it. When we believe we're going to win, our intention changes, ultimately affecting the impact of these moments. The result will be something we never could have imagined.

PUSH THROUGH WEARINESS

Perhaps you've heard the saying "life is a marathon, not a sprint." While a sprint is quick work with quick results, a marathon is a slog. Running 26.2 miles takes commitment and dedication; it means pushing your body long after your body wants to quit. No one ever gets through a marathon by going through the motions. Distance running is a feat of endurance that requires you to keep going even when you're weary. It's a good metaphor for life.

At times the daily routine gets to us, and we become weary. Weariness leads to complacency, and going through the motions becomes the default position of our hearts. Those moments require an active choice to remain engaged. Going through the motions will keep you moving, but it won't get you very far. Consider this wisdom from Paul:

> Let us not lose heart in doing good, for in due
> time we will reap if we do not grow weary.
> GALATIANS 6:9

Doing good means living as God has planned for those who are called to follow Him. Christian guys aren't called to go through the motions. They strive to give Christ-honoring attention and effort to all they do, not in an attempt to earn God's favor but to demonstrate that they love Jesus and take their mission seriously.

In what ways are you merely going through the motions? What weariness led you to this point?

What are a few key steps you can take to reengage with God's purpose? How will you evaluate your new engagement level?

Who has been in a situation similar to you? What could you learn from their refusal to go through the motions?

Close your D-Group time in prayer.

SESSION 5
NO MORE COMPROMISING YOUR INTEGRITY

JONATHAN EVANS

Once a year I take my family to the Baltimore Inner Harbor to have fun. On one occasion we saw a mannequin standing on a platform in the middle of the outdoor commons. The mannequin was dressed very colorfully, was painted from head to toe, and wore a big hat on its head. We were intrigued enough to take a closer look. As we got closer, I saw the mannequin blink. I realized at that moment it wasn't a mannequin at all. To have some fun, I decided I would do everything in my power to make the man laugh, move, or talk and break out of his stoic state. So I began to dance, tell jokes, and ask questions to make him move. However, no matter what I did, he wouldn't move. He was so focused on his responsibilities that all of my distractions seemed irrelevant.

At last a man walked onto the podium and touched the man on the shoulder. Immediately his fixed expression relaxed, and he took off his hat. Then the man who had walked onto the podium gave the former mannequin a check and said, "Job well done!" I realized the mannequin wasn't moved by my distractions because he was focused on his reward.

A lot of distractions in life try to make us move from integrity. Suffering, pain, depression, sickness, anxiety, fear, hatred, mourning, pride, and temptation can try to knock us off our stride. However, we're called to stay focused on God instead of all of the circumstances dancing around us. Although distractions will always swirl around our atmosphere, God has instructed us in His Word to be steadfast and immovable on the podium of life (see 1 Cor. 15:58). If we hold still in His Word, a day will come when God taps us on the shoulder and says, "Job well done!" In spite of the constant distractions in life, we're called to stay focused on the One who holds our reward in His hands. Think about it. Are you holding your ground on what you know to be true in spite of your circumstances?

STEADFAST AND IMMOVABLE

But thanks be to God, who gives us the victory
through our Lord Jesus Christ!
Therefore, my dear brothers, be steadfast, immovable,
always excelling in the Lord's work,
knowing that your labor in the Lord is not in vain.
1 CORINTHIANS 15:57-58 (HCSB)

The apostle Paul always grounded direction for living in a larger truth. In 1 Corinthians 15 he wrote about the resurrection of Jesus and its effects on our lives and witness. Paul's conclusion was simple. In light of the victory Jesus has given us, we must live our lives doing the Lord's work, knowing that living this way isn't in vain.

Brothers, live with integrity because Jesus died and rose again for you. Refuse to indulge the passion of your flesh. Don't cling to the ways of the world. Instead, trust in Christ, who has prepared good works for you to walk in beforehand (see Eph. 2:10). Know that the Holy Spirit empowers you in your weakness (see Rom. 8:26). Trust that when you're tempted, you have a way out (see 1 Cor. 10:13). Live with integrity because Christ has empowered you to live that way.

When are you most tempted to compromise your integrity? How do you withstand temptation in those moments?

Why is sharing an area of struggle with a trusted group of friends freeing? How can we support one another today in our struggles?

What verses of Scripture should we seek to memorize to help us overcome temptation when it arises?

Close your D-Group time in prayer.

SESSION 6
NO MORE SIFTING THROUGH THE RUBBLE

JONATHAN EVANS

In college one of my hobbies was breeding pit bulls. Pit bulls are my favorite breed of dog because of their strength, size, athleticism, and most of all, the size of their heads. The head of the pit bull is the breed's major selling point.

One day I was working in my home when I heard whining in the backyard. It sounded as if one of my dogs was badly injured. When I got out back, I found that one of my pit bulls was trying to escape. He couldn't jump over my six-foot fence, so he decided to go under it. The problem was, he didn't take into consideration the size of his head. He was stuck underneath the fence because his head was too big to go all the way through. One half of his head was outside the fence, and the other half of his head was still inside. This dog was as stuck as stuck could be. When he decided to escape from my presence and operate on his own, it proved to be a decision that got him stuck in a situation he couldn't get himself out of. There was nothing left for him to do other than call on the one from whom he was trying to escape to deliver him. My dog's greatest selling point became his greatest weakness.

Sometimes the size of our heads get us stuck in situations we can't get ourselves out of. We can become so confident that our great selling points become our great weaknesses. God is calling us to stay in the yard of humility so that we don't get stuck in the spiritual rut of self-sufficiency. Our greatest selling point as guys must be that we trust our Master and are willing to serve where He has placed us.

Think about it. Are you living your life with an oversized head?

NOT WORTH COMPARING

We do not lose heart, but though our outer man is decaying, yet our inner man is being renewed day by day. For momentary, light affliction is producing for us an eternal weight of glory far beyond all comparison,while we look not at the things which are seen, but at the things which are not seen; for the things which are seen are temporal, but the things which are not seen are eternal.

2 CORINTHIANS 4:16-18

Paul was a man who experienced a lot of hardship. Before he met Jesus, he persecuted the church and tried to destroy it. After he met Jesus, he was beaten, arrested, met with suspicion, ridiculed, and shipwrecked, among other awful things. Interestingly, we never saw Paul get fixated on those moments.

Sure, he mentioned them when he was sharing the faith but never in a "woe is me" way. His previous sin and his current hardship never caused him to take his eyes off Jesus. He acknowledged that we live in a sinful world that chips away at us day after day. However, he confidently said the rubble of this present life isn't worth comparing to the glory ahead.

If we focus on the rubble in life, we'll never see what Christ is building on a new foundation. Instead, we lift our eyes to what awaits us in eternity and focus on becoming the young men Christ is making us to be. We lay the rubble aside and focus on Jesus and the life He's preparing for us.

How can you use your past hurts to lead others to see Jesus more clearly?

Are you stuck in the rubble right now? How can you trust Christ's sufficiency to move you through it?

Who is someone you can help climb out of the rubble?

Close your D-Group time in prayer.

SESSION 7
NO MORE
HALF STEPPING

JONATHAN EVANS

You might not believe this, but the first time I dunked the basketball, I was only eleven years old. I know what you're thinking: *There's no way you dunked at eleven years old.* My father was thinking the same thing the day I ran into his office and shouted, "I dunked! I dunked! Come to the gym with me so that I can show you!"

When we got to the gym, I grabbed the basketball and told my dad to stand back. I vividly remember taking a position just above the three-point line and starting my race toward the basket. I put everything I had into leaping up as high as I could, and in the blink of an eye, BOOM! At eleven years old I dunked with authority.

When I looked at my father, however, he didn't seem to be quite as impressed as I thought he would be. He suddenly left the gym, came back a few seconds later with the head custodian, and kindly ask him to raise the goal I had dunked on from six feet to ten feet. Then my dad looked at me and said, "Son, don't be satisfied that you dunked at six feet, because that's not the standard for basketball. When you're ready to dunk at the standard ten feet, then I'll be ready to watch." I learned a valuable lesson that day. Just because I dunked didn't mean I'd met the standard.

Many men think they're doing well just because they're dunking at a cultural standard of Christianity. However, living as a kingdom man and living as a cultural man are two totally different standards. Just because the culture agrees with you doesn't mean God does. Just because you're stepping up in the eyes of the culture doesn't mean you're not half stepping in the eyes of the Father. Therefore, if your goal is to make your heavenly Father proud, you must raise the goal and dunk at a biblical standard even in a pagan culture. We've been called to be like Christ. Everything else is half stepping. Think about it. Is biblical living your standard, or are you satisfied with cultural dunking?

A FIXED HOPE

Discipline yourself for the purpose of godliness; for bodily discipline is only of little profit, but godliness is profitable for all things, since it holds promise for the present life and also for the life to come.... For it is for this we labor and strive, because we have fixed our hope on the living God, who is the Savior of all men, especially of believers.
1 TIMOTHY 4:7-8,10

Paul compared following the Lord to physical training. If someone wants to be healthy, they need to commit to exercise. If someone wants to be spiritually healthy, they must commit themselves to following the Lord.

Half stepping in our spiritual lives leads to half stepping everywhere else because all we do flows from our heart. We need to be guys who take seriously the call to follow Jesus wherever He leads. To do this, we need to commit ourselves to reading God's Word, praying, fasting, serving, giving, and loving other people.

As we develop discipline in these areas, the desire to stop half stepping in other areas will follow because our thoughts and our lives will be transformed by a God who doesn't half step. Our fixed hope on Him keeps us from half stepping in other areas.

What spiritual practices help us fix our hope on Jesus? To what spiritual practice do you need to more fully commit?

What are you currently learning about what it means to follow Jesus? Why is it beneficial to discuss these ideas with other followers of Jesus?

Confess any areas in which you're half stepping. Ask God to strengthen your resolve to give your best effort in the places He has called you.

Close your D-Group time in prayer.

SESSION 8
NO MORE STANDING ON THE SIDELINES

JONATHAN EVANS

A famous tightrope walker planned to walk a tightrope across Niagara Falls. People came from all over the world to watch this man take the walk of death across the falls on a small rope. When he got on the rope and walked across with no problem, the people cheered in awe at this amazing feat.

Then the man asked the crowd if they thought he could roll a barrel on a rope across the falls. All of the people cheered and said, "Yes! Yes! We know you can do it!" The man responded by saying, "Then who wants to get in the barrel?" The crowd immediately went from cheers to absolute silence. Everyone looked around, waiting to see who would have the courage to put their life at risk. However, no one spoke up and came forward. Although everyone believed as a spectator, no one was willing to believe as a participant.

People came from all over to witness the miraculous works of Jesus also. They stood in awe as He healed the sick, gave sight to the blind, opened the ears of the deaf, casted out demons, and perfectly fulfilled biblical prophecy. People crowded around and cheered at the sight of this incredible man.

Even in the twenty-first century, people are still crowding by the millions to celebrate Jesus Christ. In churches all over the world, people come together Sunday after Sunday to pay homage to this incredible man. With great certainty we cheer the fact that He can save, bring freedom, and deliver. However, Christ is asking for more than cheers from His people. He wants us to take risks, take up our crosses, and deny ourselves to follow Him (see Matt. 16:24). Many guys will cheer on Sunday, but few will risk following Jesus every day. Christ isn't looking for faith spectators. He's looking for faith participants. Think about it. Are you a spectator or a participant in God's kingdom agenda?

FOLLOW JESUS

When you look at the life of Jesus, you see a man who never sat still. Sure, He enjoyed meals with friends, rested, slept, and had a healthy life rhythm, but He was never passive. He involved Himself in people's lives. He healed, taught, fed, and corrected people when necessary. He spoke to outcasts. He ate with tax collectors and sinners. He comforted the family of a deceased friend. He gave His life for the sake of our salvation and for the glory of God.

Following Jesus isn't a life on the sidelines. It means denying yourself and following Him. Jesus put it this way:

> If anyone wishes to come after Me, he must deny himself, and take up his cross and follow Me. For whoever wishes to save his life will lose it; but whoever loses his life for My sake will find it.
> MATTHEW 16:24-25

Three simple instructions: deny yourself, take up His cross, follow Him. We are called to live as people who have no interest but the interest of our Father in heaven. We are called to embrace the cross of Christ as the center of our salvation and the guiding point of our lives. We must follow Jesus wherever He leads. Young men, Jesus will never lead you to stay on the sidelines. If you follow His voice, you'll always be in the game.

Where is Jesus leading you right now? Are you following Him?

In what ways are you sidelined? What needs to change? How can we hold one another accountable?

What's your most significant takeaway from this Bible study?

Close your D-Group time in prayer.

MY DISCIPLESHIP GROUP

You can walk through this Bible study on your own, but we aren't meant to walk with Jesus alone. This is a great opportunity to bring together 2-4 of your friends to form a discipleship group (also known as a D-Group). Use this Bible study as a method of going through God's Word together, then challenge each other to live out what you read through discussion, accountability, and prayer. Don't forget to have fun together while doing it.

Who's in your group? Write their names below.

What are 2-3 goals you want to set as a group for this next year?

1

2

3

PRAYER REQUESTS

Keep a record of any major prayer requests from your D-Group on this page. Write down the request, the person who asked for prayer, and the date. See what God does in and through your group this year.

DATE	PERSON & PRAYER REQUEST

SOURCES

Session 1

1. Malcolm Gladwell, *Outliers: The Story of Success* (Boston: Little, Brown, 2011).

Session 3

1. Jennifer Allen, "Nixon's Tricks Not in Redskins' Playbook," *ESPN* [online], [accessed August 30, 2021]. Available from the internet: https://www.espn.com/page2/wash/s/allen/020308.html.

Session 6

1. "Michael Jordan," *BrainyQuote* [online], [accessed February 25, 2019]. Available from the internet: https://www.brainyquote.com/quotes/michael_jordan_127660.